Rising Sun
Echoes Of The Damned

Satori Saru

CONTENTS

Rising Sun: Echoes of the damned

Acknowledgments

In the weaving of this tapestry of imagination, I find myself indebted to a multitude of individuals who have contributed their energy, wisdom, and support to bring these words to life. To each of you, I extend my heartfelt gratitude:

My Muse: To the wellspring of inspiration that whispers in the corners of creativity, thank you for guiding my pen through the realms of fantasy and wonder.

My wife, Christina: For your unwavering encouragement, understanding during late-night writing sessions, and the joyous celebrations in the triumphs, thank you for being my anchor.

Literary Community: To fellow writers, mentors, and readers who share a passion for storytelling, thank you for fostering a community where ideas flourish, and creativity knows no bounds.

Readers: To those who embark on this journey through the pages, your curiosity and engagement breathe life into these words. Your presence in this adventure is the ultimate honor.

This book is a testament to the collaborative spirit that fuels the world of storytelling. This page represents a spark that ignited the flame of my imagination. May the echoes of our shared journey resonate far and wide.

With deepest gratitude,

Satori Saru

CHAPTER 1
AWAKENING SHADOWS

The celestial dance of the stars seemed choreographed by the cosmos itself, as if they were penning an ode to the majesty of the night. A gray moon, cleaved neatly by the dark line of the horizon, cast a ghostly glow over the world below. Jupiter's transit, a bright wanderer in the heavens, traced a luminescent trail to the ancient Chinese temple, its silhouette etched against the indigo tapestry of the sky.

"Each stone of this mountain," Sifu's voice began, low and resonant, "has been witness to the passage of countless moons." His eyes, reflecting millennia of knowledge, fixed upon the faces that encircled him under the broad canopy of the bonsai. Its twisted limbs stretched above them like protective arms, cradling them in a sanctuary of wisdom.

"Legends," he breathed out, his chest rising with the weight of history, "are not merely tales we tell. They are the essence of our spirit; the very breath of our ancestors."

The students, clad in simple brown and tan robes that whispered with each subtle movement, leaned forward, their bodies taut with anticipation. In the flickering light of the red lanterns, which swayed gently as if to the rhythm of Sifu's intonation, their shadows intermingled, creating a tapestry of eager disciples hungry for enlightenment.

"Listen to the river," Sifu gestured toward the sound of water slicing through the heart of the temple, its journey a mirror of life—twisting, turning, sometimes turbulent. It flowed from the source, only to leap courageously from the precipice, transforming into a waterfall that roared with the ferocity of nature's will. "It tells a story of persistence, of sacrifice."

A murmur of agreement rippled through the group. Quon, whose gaze was the most intense among them, felt the resonance of the master's words within his own chest—a drumbeat that marched in time with the pulsing waterfall.

"Heroism," Sifu continued, the word hanging in the air like a promise, "is born from such sacrifice. From the willingness to give all for something greater than oneself."

Quon's hands clenched into fists at his sides. He knew of sacrifice; his dreams were drenched in it, haunted by the specter of loss.

"Courage," Sifu's voice dipped, coaxing them to delve deeper, "does not always roar. Sometimes, it is the quiet voice at the end of the day that says, 'I will try again tomorrow.'"

"Redemption," Sifu said, locking eyes with each student in turn, "awaits those who are brave enough to seek it."

And as the night embraced the temple in its star-studded cloak, Quon understood that his path was one of many threads in the fabric of this ancient tale—a narrative woven through generations, where every stitch was a step towards the ultimate triumph of light over darkness.

"Listen closely, my dear students," Sifu began, his voice low and resonant against the hush of twilight. "For today, I shall share with you the legend of Sun Wukong, the tyrant who sought to overthrow the order of the light and plunge the world into darkness."

Quon leaned in with rapt attention, his eyes fixed on Sifu as the last rays of sunlight danced across the wise man's weathered face. The very air seemed to thicken with anticipation, and a shiver of unease rippled through him.

"Long ago, in a time when the world was a different place, Sun Wukong rose to power," Sifu continued, his eyes narrowing as if he could see the past unfold before him. "He was no ordinary warrior; he was an immortal which possessed unmatched strength, agility, and cunning."

The students exchanged anxious glances. Quon could feel their collective tension—the same fear that clawed at his insides. It was more than a story; it was a specter from a past that refused to die.

"With a legion of warriors at his command," Sifu said, his hands moving like graceful birds, "he embarked on a campaign to conquer the lands and spread darkness."

In the dimming light, shadows crept along the ground like dark tendrils reaching out to ensnare them. Quon imagined the immortal Sun Wukong, a figure so daunting that even the bravest hearts faltered in his presence.

Sweat beaded on Quon's brow, not from the heat, but from the weight of a destiny he felt bound to fulfill. His father had stood against such darkness, a bulwark of bravery and sacrifice. Could he muster the same courage?

A breeze stirred the leaves of the bonsai, and the red lanterns swayed gently, casting an ominous glow. Quon's fists tightened, knuckles whitening. The legend was not just a cautionary tale; it was a clarion call to arms for all who sat under Sifu's tutelage.

"Darkness covered the land like a suffocating blanket," Sifu whispered, almost to himself, "and despair took root in the hearts of men."

Quon's heart raced. He envisioned legions clashing, the clang of steel upon steel, the cries of the fallen echoing through time. His own fears battled within him—fears of inadequacy, fears of failing those who had come before him.

"Yet, where there is shadow, there must also be light," Sifu declared, his voice rising with conviction. "And it is we who must be the bearers of that light."

Quon exhaled slowly, letting the words seep into him. Sun Wukong may have been a scourge upon the earth, but he was also the anvil upon which heroes were forged. In the quiet of his mind, a resolve took shape, as unyielding as the mountain upon which they sat.

"Remember this," Sifu said, locking eyes with Quon, "the mightiest power lies not in strength or speed, but in the indomitable will of the spirit."

Quon met Sifu's gaze, feeling the truth of his words resonate deep within his core. His father's sacrifice would not be in vain. He would rise and train harder, become faster, smarter—whatever it took to honor his lineage and keep the light alive.

Sifu's voice seemed to merge with the rustling leaves of the ancient bonsai, whispering secrets as darkness loomed like a living thing over the lands. "Individuals from all corners of the earth were chosen to come to this very temple," he gestured grandly, his sleeve sweeping like a painter's brush against the air, revealing the hulking silhouette of the sacred structure.

The moonlight carved his features as he continued, "To be trained as apprentice monks and molded into great samurais, the defenders of light against the encroaching darkness." The red lanterns flickered as if in agreement, casting their glow on the eager faces around him.

Quon felt the weight of those words settle upon his shoulders like the heavy mantle of destiny. His gaze swept across his companions—faces from distant lands, each marked by the rich tapestry of their heritage. Jade nodded solemnly, her dark eyes alight with the fire of purpose. Beside her, Hakana whose hair was the color of the wheat fields at sunrise clenched his jaw, resolve etched into his fair complexion.

"Every strike of your hand, every chant from your lips, it weaves you into the fabric of history," Sifu said, locking eyes with each student in turn. Quon felt the intensity of that gaze, and within him, something responded—a spark ready to ignite.

His thoughts churned, churning like the river that bisected the temple grounds. He was part of something greater, a lineage of warriors who had stood where he now sat, who had faced the darkness with nothing but their spirit and a blade. It was a legacy that demanded everything and promised only the chance for honor.

"Your training is not merely for combat," Sifu intoned, breaking through Quon's reverie. "It is to become the very essence of what we fight for—to embody the light."

Quon nodded, feeling the truth of Sifu's words resonate within him. His fists clenched involuntarily as he thought of his father, his family, and the life that had been torn from him. The shadows of past nightmares threatened to creep into his heart, but he pushed them away, focusing instead on the here and now—the soft whisper of silk robes, the distant echo of the waterfall, the collective breath of his fellow apprentices.

"But there was more to this tale," Sifu continued, the timbre of his voice sinking into a hushed tone that begged for closer attention.

Quon leaned in, along with the others, as if by mere inches they could draw nearer to the legend itself. The moonlight caught in Sifu's eyes, turning them into pools of liquid silver, reflecting a resolve that had been tempered by time and trial.

"A legend told of a special weapon," he intoned, "a blade forged with the power to slay a god and vanquish any immortal, like Sun Wukong himself. It was said that this weapon could tip the scales of the war in our favor."

Quon's hand absentmindedly traced the floor beneath him, imagining the feel of such a weapon in his grasp—the weight, the balance, the undeniable force it would carry. His heart raced with the possibility of wielding power so great that the very heavens might bend at its command.

"Brave warriors from this temple," Sifu said, his gaze sweeping across his students, as if peering into the depth of their souls, "ventured forth, journeying to the farthest reaches of the earth in search of this divine blade."

Quon's mind conjured images of treacherous peaks, vast deserts, and untamed seas. Each landscape a canvas upon which the valor of these warriors was etched.

"They faced trials and tribulations," Sifu's voice held a cadence that matched the beat of Quon's heart, "but their resolve remained unwavering, for the fate of the world rested upon their shoulders."

A shiver ran down Quon's spine, not from the chill of the night, but from the knowledge that he, too, could be called upon to follow in such footsteps.

"Each step they took was a testament to their courage," Sifu spoke, his words painting a tapestry of struggle and determination, "and though many sought the blade, it was understood that only the purest of heart might ever lay hands upon it."

Quon felt the weight of his own doubts and fears, wondering if his heart could be counted among the pure. He glanced around at his fellow apprentices, seeing his own apprehension mirrored in their eyes. Yet, there was also a glint of hope—a shared understanding that they were bound by something greater than themselves.

"Let their journey be your inspiration," Sifu urged them, his voice now barely above a whisper, yet it resonated with the power of a thunderclap. "For you are the next generation of warriors who will defend all that is sacred and just in this world."

"Rest now," Sifu concluded, his presence a comforting balm to their heightened senses. "Tomorrow, we continue our daily training, with hearts brave and minds sharp. The path of a samurai is never easy, but it is noble and true."

The moon, now a pale guardian in the ink-black sky, cast its silvery gaze upon a congregation of students whose faces were etched with a tapestry of cultures and nations. They sat before Sifu, their bodies as still as the ancient bonsai that spread its gnarled limbs over them like a protective embrace. Yet within each student's chest, hearts beat with a purpose as enduring as the mountain on which they trained.

Quon felt his muscles tense, not from the day's exertions but from the electricity of anticipation that crackled through the air. He watched as Sifu's shadow danced across the temple stones, a manifestation of the tales woven into the fabric of their lives. When the elder's eyes met his, Quon saw the reflection of countless dawns and dusks that had witnessed the rise and fall of warriors.

Sifu nodded at him, a silent acknowledgment that spoke volumes. "As we stand here today," he concluded, his words resonating with the solemnity of an oath, "the war continues. Sun Wukong presses on with his dark ambitions, but we, the defenders of light, shall not falter."

Quon exchanged determined glances with his fellow apprentices, each pair of eyes alight with the shared flame of conviction. They understood—they were the bulwark against the tide of shadows threatening to engulf their world.

"We shall train tirelessly," Sifu's voice wove through the stillness, "uphold the honor of our ancestors, and protect the world from the looming darkness."

"Remember this tale, my students," he implored, every syllable steeped in the gravity of their heritage, "for it is a reminder of our purpose and the legacy we carry forward."

"Goodnight, Sifu," echoed through the dusk as the pupils, one by one, bowed low with a reverence that spoke volumes of their respect.

"Goodnight, my students," Sifu replied, his voice a soft hum that rode the gentle breeze. "May your dreams be visited by the wisdom of our ancestors."

"Let us honor the sacrifices made for us," Quon said softly to his closest comrades, his voice steady despite the turmoil that raged like a storm beneath his calm exterior.

"Let us be worthy of the legends that birthed us," Hakana replied, his eyes reflecting the starlight and the unspoken bond that tethered them to one another.

They dispersed to their sleeping corridor, a large room with bamboo mats aligned on the floor. As Quon lay on his bamboo mat, the scent of incense a gentle balm to his spirit, he closed his eyes and envisioned the dawn. He saw himself standing on the mountain peak, divine sword in hand, ready to carve a path for those who would follow.

With the sounds of his fellow pupils' steady breathing lulling him toward slumber, Quon allowed himself a moment's reprieve from vigilance. "Tomorrow, we train anew," he reaffirmed within his quiet thoughts. "With hearts brave and minds sharp." He repeated his mantra until falling asleep.

The stillness of the night was shattered by a cacophony of terror, wrenching the boy from his dreams. His heart pounded against his ribs as if it sought escape, each beat a drum of dread in the silence that followed. He lay there, a statue under his thin covers, eyes wide in the dark. The muffled cries of his parents seeped through the paper-thin walls, urgent and fearful.

"Shh, stay quiet," he whispered to himself, a silent prayer for safety. A floorboard creaked somewhere beyond his door, and with it, the illusion of peace crumbled.

He lays still trying to distinguish the sounds but his fear increases when he hears his mother running for her youngest child's bedroom, her feet pattering in the distance.

"Come on, son!" The deep tone of his father's voice was laced with an unfamiliar tremor as he stood at the doorway of the child's bedroom, and in the dim moonlight, the boy saw the sword in his father's hand—a silver streak of determination.

Tentatively, the boy slid his feet to the cool floor, mustering the courage of warriors from stories told.

But then—like a specter—a dark figure loomed, materializing out of the shadows behind his father. With a swift, brutal movement, the katana pierced flesh and fabric alike, the cruel sound of rending life a scream in the hush.

Blood curdled in his throat as he stumbled back onto his bed, a strangled cry escaping his lips even as his father crumpled to the ground—a puppet severed from its strings.

"Father!" It was more than a word; it was the shattering of his world.

Violence had erupted like a storm across his village, washing away innocence and leaving chaos in its wake. As he was seized by the stranger, the boy thrashed wildly, his small frame surging with a primal need to survive.

"Let me go!" he spat, but the words were swallowed by the night.

A cloth, heavy with the scent of chemicals, smothered his protests, pressed against his face by hands with the strength of iron bands. His lungs screamed for air, a fire igniting within his chest. Through the haze of fear and suffocation, the terrified wails of his mother and the anguished cries of his brother clawed at his consciousness, a haunting serenade to his helplessness.

"Mother! Brother!" he tried to call out, but darkness encroached, eager to claim him.

The world dimmed, sounds and struggles fading into nothingness. And as the last light of awareness flickered and died, the boy surrendered to the void that beckoned, a silent witness to the unseen war.

Quon's eyelids flew open, catapulting him from the clutches of his nightmare into the silent dormitory. His heart galloped against his ribs, a relentless drumbeat in the stillness. Moonlight slipped through the paper screens, draping over his quivering form, and casting an ethereal glow on the droplets of sweat that clung to his forehead. He swallowed hard; the taste of fear thick in his mouth.

"Easy... just a dream," he whispered to himself, though the tremor in his voice betrayed his attempt at reassurance. With care, he lifted the weight of his blanket and placed bare feet upon the cool bamboo floor. The mats seemed to hold their breath as he moved, refusing to betray his passage with even the slightest creak.

He paused, his gaze sweeping over his fellow students. Their chests rose and fell in the rhythm of deep sleep, untouched by the tumult of Quon's inner world. He envied them that peace. With measured steps, he glided towards the sliding door that separated them from the night.

The courtyard greeted him with a wash of tranquility. Cherry trees whispered secrets to the breeze, their branches framing the heavens above. Stars twinkled, serene observers to the turmoil within Quon's soul, and he couldn't help but wonder if they held the answers he sought.

"Father," he breathed out, the word a ghost on his lips. "I wish you could see this." The memory of blood and steel flashed before his eyes, unbidden, and he shook his head as if to dispel the image.

He wrapped his arms around himself, the cool wind kissing his cheeks and playing with the hem of his sleeping robe. It was as if nature itself sought to soothe him, the caress almost maternal in its gentleness.

"Courage, Quon. Have courage," he murmured, drawing strength from the vastness above. His father had taught him to find solace in the stars, to look up when the weight of the world bowed his shoulders. Yet now, it was not the weight of the world, but the specter of his past that threatened to crush him.

"Will I ever be free of you?" he questioned the darkness, his voice barely a whisper. The stars offered no reply, maintaining their vigil in silent solidarity.

"Am I destined to be haunted?" His thoughts roamed, seeking refuge from the relentless memories. They were like shadows, always lurking at the edge of his consciousness, ready to pounce the moment his guard dropped.

"Is this my fate?" His hands clenched into fists at his sides, the frustration simmering beneath the surface. He had come here to train, to become strong, to forge a path that honored his family. Yet, the past clung to him with the persistence of a shadow.

The tranquility of the night was a stark contrast to the chaos churning within Quon. He had sought solace in the courtyard's embrace, where shadows played across ancient stones and whispered secrets of a time-worn peace. The cherry trees swayed gently, like silent guardians keeping watch over his troubled spirit.

"Bad dream, Quon?" The voice, unexpectedly present in the stillness, was soft yet carried an undeniable strength.

Quon turned sharply, his heart skipping a beat. In the moonlight, Sifu's presence was almost ethereal, an anchor of serenity amidst the sea of Quon's inner disorder. The elder sat rooted in meditation, his hands forming an unbreakable bond, his being the very embodiment of calm that Quon so desperately yearned for.

With a simple nod, Quon acknowledged the nightmare that had torn him from sleep, his throat constricted with the effort of pushing down emotions too raw, too potent. "Yes, Sifu," he managed to say, the words barely more than a breath.

The air around them seemed to hum with the energy of unspoken understanding, the connection between master and student transcending the need for further words.

Sifu's eyes opened, revealing depths of empathy and experience that drew Quon in, inviting him to unburden his soul. But Quon hesitated, caught between the vulnerability of confession and the stoicism he believed a samurai should embody.

"Let it out, young warrior," Sifu encouraged, his voice a grounding force. "The shadows of the mind can only be dispelled by the light of acknowledgment."

Quon's fists unclenched as he allowed the walls he had built to crumble, piece by piece. His breath shuddered as the images replayed in his mind—the violent end of innocence, the cold grip of fear, the helplessness that haunted him.

Under the luminous gaze of the half-sliced moon, the elder monk's silhouette merged with the night, a guardian spirit carved from stillness itself. Sifu's eyes, deep pools of ancient knowledge, never left Quon as the boy recounted his recurring nightmare.

"Every time I close my eyes," Quon started, the words gaining momentum as if breaking free from a dam within him, "it's there—the past, the pain... It doesn't feel like just a dream. It feels like..." His voice trailed off, lost in the echoes of memories that refused to be silenced.

Sifu's voice was a low thrum, harmonious with the distant waterfall's cascade. "That does sound like quite the nightmare."

Sifu watched the boy carefully, reading the play of emotions on his pupil's face. There was sorrow there, and fear, but also a burgeoning strength that had yet to fully surface. "Your past shapes you, Quon, but it does not define you," Sifu said softly.

"Could it be a sign? A message I'm meant to decipher?" Quon asked, searching Sifu's face for a glimpse of enlightenment. His own visage, young yet marred by early shadows of suffering, searched for a path through the veils of sleep-induced terror.

"Signs are often the language of our subconscious," Sifu offered, his tone a needlepoint woven with threads of comfort and sagacity. "Unravel their meaning, and you may find the clarity you seek."

Sifu's sigh whispered through the cool night air, resonating with an ancient fatigue that seemed to seep from the very stones of the temple. "Quon," he said softly, his voice like the rustle of leaves in a sacred grove, "the mind is both sanctuary and battlefield. What you've dreamt may not be mere shadows but echoes... echoes of a past trauma."

Quon felt the truth in Sifu's words settle in his chest like a heavy stone. His eyes reflected the turmoil within—a tempest swirling with images of fire and steel. He swallowed hard, the taste of fear still lingering on his tongue.

"Since childhood, I have walked these halls, participated in countless battles, Sifu," Quon murmured, his gaze drifting towards the temple's silhouette against the starry backdrop. "My days are filled with the clangor of blades and the mantras of discipline. Is it not my destiny to follow the path of honor, to become one of temple's most noble samurais?"

"Destiny is crafted by our choices," Sifu replied, his eyes as deep and unfathomable as the night sky. "And this temple—this cradle of warriors—is where choices forge spirits stronger than any blade."

"Tomorrow's dawn will find me stronger," Quon promised himself, feeling the embers of his resolve glow brighter within. He bowed deeply to Sifu, a silent pledge to honor the sacrifices made for him— to rise above the ashes of his haunted past and embrace the mantle of protector that awaited him.

"Good," Sifu acknowledged with a nod. "For in the dance of combat and the quietude of reflection, you will discover the true essence of a samurai. Now rest, Quon. The morrow awaits."

As Quon retreated to the dormitory, the incense-infused breeze carried whispers of encouragement from the ancestors who had once walked these sacred grounds. In their ethereal chorus, he found a steadfast encouragement, guiding him towards the dawning light of a new day.

His bamboo mat awaited him, a humble abode of rest within the communal dormitory. As he approached his mat, he saw a figure standing in the shadows. Quons heart raced as he grabbed his sword and prepared to defend himself. But as the figure stepped closer, he recognized the face of his closest friend, Hakana.

Moonlight danced in his eyes, which searched Quon's face for an answer, reflecting a brotherhood that ran deeper than blood.

Hakana took a step forward, closing the distance between them. His posture relaxed slightly, though his gaze remained piercing, seeking the truth that lay beneath Quon's composed exterior. "You shouldn't wander alone at night; rules exist for our safety," he admonished, though his tone held less reproach and more the weight of genuine concern for his friend's well-being.

Quon went on to tell Hakana of his dream and that he just needed fresh air from the courtyard.

"Again?" The concern in Hakana's voice was not tinged with judgment but laced with the empathy of shared hardships.

"Sleep has been elusive," he continued, acknowledging the dark circles that had taken up residence under his eyes. "Each night is a journey through shadows, and each morning I return more tired than before." Quon echoed.

Hakana placed his hand upon Quon's shoulder, the stillness of the night wrapped around them, a silent embrace that held at bay the restive world beyond the temple gates.

"Let's get some rest," Hakana said softly, his voice barely more than a whisper woven into the night's arras. "Morning will be here before we know it."

In sync with each other's movements, they crossed the cool wooden floor, the echo of their footfalls solemn as a whispered mantra. Each mat lay parallel, an unrolled scroll of solace in the dimly lit chamber.

As they neared the bamboo mats that would cradle their bodies until dawn, Quon allowed himself one last look skyward through the window. He wondered if the ancestors, too, had marveled at the constellations, drawing strength from their unwavering light. With a deep inhale, he embraced the quiet assurance that no matter where their paths led, the stars would remain as witnesses to their enduring alliance.

"May our spirits be as resilient as the night," Quon mused inwardly, a silent prayer for the trials ahead.

"Always," came Hakana's soft echo, as if in answer to the unspoken wish.

They covered up and laid their heads to rest.

A soft aroma of incense filled the night air, carrying with it hints of sandalwood and vanilla. It was an earthy scent that soothed any unease, making it easy to drift off into a deep slumber.

CHAPTER 2
ENCHANTED CHAINS

The deep, sonorous gong resonated through the stone walls of the temple, its sound a forceful herald of daybreak. With a vibrational embrace, it awakened Quon from his slumber along with his fellow students, the familiar timbre pulling him from the realm of dreams into the discipline of dawn. He rose from his modest bedding, a thin mat on the cold floor, as did Hakana in the bed adjacent. They exchanged silent nods, acknowledging the day's start with the same mutual understanding they had shared since childhood.

"Another day to forge our spirits," Quon murmured, his voice a whisper amongst the stirring of monks.

"Through steel and silence," Hakana replied, the mantra of their order.

They moved in unison, feet padding softly across the wooden floors as they joined the stream of bodies flowing towards the courtyard. The air was crisp, the first light of morning painting everything with a golden touch that made even the austere temple seem aglow. Quon felt the quiet energy within him stir, the breath in his lungs syncing with the rhythmic steps of his fellow disciples.

As they entered the courtyard, their Sifu commanded immediate attention. His presence was as much a part of the dawn as the sun itself, casting long shadows over the dew-kissed grass. The statues of ancient warriors seemed to bow in respect around him, and the shrubs shivered slightly in the breeze, as if in anticipation of the wisdom he would impart.

"Discipline is our path; repetition our guide," Sifu intoned, eyes closed, hands clasped before him in unwavering serenity. The Bhairava Mudra symbolized his inner strength, something Quon aspired to mirror.

Quon felt the stern gaze of Sifu even with the elder's eyes closed, as if he could see through eyelids and into the depths of his soul. It was both comforting and unnerving, and he swallowed the lump that formed in his throat, determined to show no weakness.

"Today, let your movements reflect your intent," Sifu said, opening his eyes, which settled upon each disciple in turn. "Let the mind be as fluid as the body."

"Yes, Sifu," came the chorus of voices, Quon's among them.

The morning light, now a golden cascade of warmth, cast an ethereal glow over the temple's inner courtyard. As Quon and Hakana assumed their positions on the dew-kissed grass, they watched as Sifu stood motionless, the embodiment of tranquility. Yet, it was impossible to miss the single sword that hung at his waist, its hilt adorned with intricate carvings of dragons and phoenixes. The blade, unsheathed for a mere moment, captured the sun's rays, reflecting a dance of light across the cobblestones.

Quon felt the familiar grip of reverence tighten around his chest. To bear witness to such stillness in Sifu was to understand the latent power that lay beneath—the kind forged through lifetimes of mastery. With every slow inhalation, Sifu drew not just air, but the very essence of the ancient traditions into his lungs. Exhaling, it seemed as if he were bestowing upon them the collected wisdom of generations past.

"Let us begin!" Sifu's command echoed like thunder, snapping Quon back from his reverie. The master clapped his hands twice, a sharp sound that cut cleanly through the morning stillness.

Sifu's silhouette, a dark shape against the dawning light, moved through the assembly of students with the silent grace of a drifting shadow. The hem of his gi whispered across the stone floor as he navigated the space between each disciple, his presence a calm yet commanding force in the morning ritual.

"Deeper," Sifu's voice was a soft command, reaching the ears of a novice whose stance wavered like a reed in the wind. The student's eyes widened as two fingers, firm yet gentle, pressed upon his shoulder, guiding him to lower his center of gravity. "The earth is your ally," Sifu murmured, his tone imbued with the wisdom of countless sunrises spent in practice and contemplation.

Quon watched from the corner of his eye, noting the subtle correction, an inward reminder to ground himself further. His legs tensed, pushing against the invisible force that sought to uproot him. He could feel Hakana's energy beside him, a focused intensity that mirrored his own determination.

"Better," Sifu praised, his words floating through the air like leaves on a gentle stream. He continued on, a shepherd among his flock, ensuring each one was aligned.

With deliberate steps, Sifu approached Quon and Hakana. Quon felt a flush of warmth in his chest, an ember of pride glowing at the prospect of Sifu's scrutiny. They executed a series of forms, their movements synchronized without need for spoken cues. This dance of combat, a language of its own, conveyed messages of strength, control, and unity.

A low hum rumbled from Sifu's throat, resonating like a chord struck on an ancient instrument. It was a sound of approval that vibrated within Quon's very bones, affirming their dedication. The acknowledgment served as a beacon, illuminating the path they walked—one paved by the relentless pursuit of mastery.

Retreating to the heart of the courtyard, Sifu's footsteps left no trace, as if he glided over the very air itself. Quon allowed himself a momentary breath of relief. 'To earn Sifu's praise,' he thought, 'is to touch the sublime.'

"Focus, brother," Hakana whispered, a private mantra shared between them.

"Always," Quon replied through gritted teeth, sweat carving rivulets down his temple. His mind's eye held the image of the sword at Sifu's side—a symbol of the discipline that coursed through their veins.

"Remember," Sifu called out to all, his voice carrying the weight of tradition, "the truest blade is forged not in fire, but in the stillness of resolve."

Quon internalized the words, feeling them etch into his consciousness. Each position he held, every controlled exhale, was a testament to the unspoken vow he had taken—the commitment to embody the principles that bound them as warriors of this venerable order.

Quon's muscles were a symphony of motion, each movement flowing into the next as he practiced his katas with Hakana. The clack of bamboo echoed through the courtyard, a rhythm that pulsed like the heartbeat of the temple itself. Each strike was precise, a testament to hours of dedication and pain.

"Extend fully," Quon urged Hakana under his breath, parrying a thrust. "Like Sifu says, reach beyond the target."

"Right," Hakana grunted in response, his brow furrowed in concentration as he adjusted his stance.

The sun climbed higher, its rays filtering through the leaves, casting dappled shadows on the ground. Sweat trailed down Quon's face, but he welcomed the warmth against his skin, a reminder of the fire within him, the drive to exceed his past self.

As they transitioned to self-defense techniques, Quon paired up with Jade, her presence a silent challenge. He respected her fluidity, the way she moved with deceptive ease. They bowed to each other, an acknowledgment of the battle to come.

"Remember, yield to redirect," Jade said, locking eyes with Quon as they began. Her voice was steady, a thread of steel beneath the calm surface.

Quon nodded, internalizing her advice. His mind replayed Sifu's lessons, seeking the balance between yielding and asserting. 'The dance of combat,' he thought, 'is one of give and take.'

"Good!" Jade exclaimed as Quon executed a seamless joint lock, dropping her to the grass with a muted thud. "You're not holding back."

"Nor are you," Quon replied, helping her up. There was a spark of pride in his chest; he could feel his skills sharpening, honed by the whetstone of relentless practice.

They continued, their bodies moving with a fierce focus that mirrored the intensity of the training around them. Quon felt the unity in this shared struggle, a bond forged by common purpose.

The relentless sun had finally begun its descent, painting the sky in shades of amber and mauve. Quon's shadow stretched across the ground, elongating as if trying to pull itself away from the exhaustion that gripped his body. His muscles ached with a fierce burn, each movement an echo of the day's rigorous training.

Students continued moving in sync, their bamboo swords clashing in a rhythmic dance, Quon's senses sharpened. He could hear the faint rustle of leaves, the gentle cadence of distant chanting, and the steady thud of his own heart, thunderous in his ears.

"Time!" The gong's sonorous call reverberated off the temple walls, its deep tone signaling the end of the day's exertions. A collective sigh rippled through the courtyard, a symphony of relief and anticipation for the evening repast.

"Finally," Hakana exhaled, sheathing his sword with an exaggerated flourish. "I'm famished."

"Race you to the washroom?" Quon teased, the corners of his mouth tilting upward despite the weariness that clung to him like a second skin.

"You're on."

Their laughter filled the air as they sprinted towards the washroom, the weight of the day momentarily forgotten. Inside, they split into their respective changing rooms, the carved bamboo dividers standing sentinel over their privacy. Soft fabric panels swayed gently as Quon passed by, the vibrant colors a stark contrast to the austere dojo.

Alone, Quon peeled off his sweat-soaked gi, the heavy fabric clinging stubbornly to his skin. Under the cascade of cool water, he let the tension wash away, droplets tracing paths along his toned frame. 'Discipline and repetition,' he reflected, echoing the elder monks' teachings, 'but also rejuvenation.'

"Looking sharp," Hakana commented as Quon emerged in his hanfu, the warm orange fabric hugging his form comfortably. The cashew overlay added a touch of elegance, the light brown trim a silent testament to their dedication.

They shared a smile, their camaraderie as woven into their being as the threads of their garments. Together, they stepped out of the washroom, ready to face the next part of their routine: dinner among friends and the warm embrace of communal sustenance.

"Today was good," Quon said, breaking the comfortable silence. "You pushed hard, Hakana."

Quon inhaled the cool, early evening air, a welcome reprieve after the day's exertions within the dojo's walls. A gentle breeze caressed his skin, still tingling from the fresh water of the washroom.

"Can you feel it?" he asked Hakana, who walked beside him beneath a canopy of cherry blossoms. "The way the world seems to pause before nightfall?"

"Like it's taking a deep breath," Hakana agreed, his eyes tracing the flutter of petals caught in the wind—a whispering dance of pink on the threshold of night.

Their steps were quiet, a silent procession along the winding paths etched with the wisdom of countless footsteps that had come before them. The sun made its descent toward the horizon, its rays casting elongated shadows that stretched across the ground like dark fingers reaching for the coming night.

Quon felt a kinship with the fading light, an empathy for its daily surrender to the darkness. "It's beautiful, isn't it? How every day ends with a burst of color, as if to say 'remember me.'"

Hakana nodded, his face illuminated by the golden hues that wrapped around them. "It's a promise," he spoke softly, "that no matter what, there's beauty at the end of the struggle."

"Perhaps that's what Sifu means when he talks about finding harmony." Quon's thoughts danced with the possibility, the concept rooted deeply within their teachings—balance even in transition, strength found in the softness of a petal's fall.

"Harmony," Hakana mused, "A delicate thing, hard-won and easily lost."

"Exactly." Quon's voice was barely above a whisper, his mind wandering to the discipline they all shared, the unspoken bond that connected each student within the temple.

With a shared glance, they ascended the stone stairs, each step echoing in the hush of early evening. At the top, Jade and Kaleb awaited, their lively conversation spilling over the last step like a welcome wave.

"Ah, there you are!" Jade exclaimed, her almond-shaped eyes sparkling with the day's triumphs. "We were beginning to think you'd gotten lost in the maze of corridors."

"Or maybe captivated by the cherry blossoms again," Kaleb chimed in, his voice rich with mirth.

Kaleb's presence commanded the open space at the top of the stairway. The last rays of sunlight painted highlights in his dirty blonde hair, giving him a halo effect that seemed fitting for his statuesque build. He was a striking contrast to the temple's native disciples—with a stature carved from different lands and a spirit that carried the untamed essence of the far west.

"Perhaps a bit of both," Quon admitted, his lips curving into a smile. "The dojo grounds have a way of holding you captive with their beauty."

"Especially when the setting sun hits just right," Hakana said, nodding towards the horizon where light danced upon the pond, turning the surface into a tapestry of gold and shadow.

Jade's laughter, light and musical, filled the space between them. "Come, let's not keep the feast waiting." Her hanfu, mirroring Kaleb's in style, swayed gracefully as she turned to lead the way.

"Indeed," Kaleb agreed. "I've heard rumors of extra helpings of dumplings tonight."

"Rumors that you started, no doubt," Hakana quipped, falling into step beside him.

"Guilty," Kaleb confessed, but his tone held no remorse. Instead, it bubbled with the zest of someone who found joy even in the smallest of daily rituals.

Quon watched them for a moment, their easy camaraderie a testament to the bonds formed within these ancient walls. As students of the temple, they shared more than just routines; they shared dreams, struggles, and the relentless pursuit of mastery over self.

Their laughter faded into the hallowed echo of the grand dining hall's entrance as they crossed its threshold, leaving behind the day's labor for the night's nourishment.

The clatter of crockery and the rustle of robes provided a harmonious backdrop to the grand dining hall as Quon entered, his senses immediately enveloped by the rich aroma that filled the vast space. The scent of jasmine rice, its grains fluffy and distinct, mingled with the earthiness of simmering broth, carrying with it the vibrant essence of garden-fresh vegetables. Steam rose in gentle wisps from clay pots and wooden bowls, curling upwards toward the high, beamed ceiling before dissipating into the sacred air.

"Ah, that's the smell of heaven," Quon murmured to himself, his stomach tightening with anticipation. His mouth watered at the thought of the warm meal soon to cascade over his tongue, a well-earned reward for the day's physical exertions.

"More like the reward for a hard day's practice, eh?" Kaleb's voice boomed beside him, his accent tinged with the exotic cadences of his distant homeland.

Quon glanced at Kaleb, noting the way the newcomer's eyes shone with the same determined light they held during training. It had only been six months since Kaleb joined their ranks, yet his presence had already altered the fabric of their daily rituals. Before Kaleb's arrival, silence was a sacred companion to their communal meals, an unspoken agreement to honor the nourishment provided to them. Now, there was an undercurrent of eagerness—a subtle shift towards camaraderie that transcended the act of eating.

"Indeed," Quon replied, the corners of his lips lifting. "Though I hardly remember what it's like to eat without the sound of your stories filling the room."

"Stories are just another kind of sustenance, my friend," Kaleb said, a teasing glint in his eyes. He moved with ease through the throng of students, his broad frame parting the crowd like a ship slicing through calm waters.

Quon followed, observing how the other students gravitated toward Kaleb's energy, drawn to the novelty he brought to their disciplined lives. His own thoughts, however, were a tangled mass. Was this change a mere ripple on the surface, or the beginning of a tide that would wash away their traditions?

"Sometimes, silence is its own story," Quon mused inwardly, taking his place at the long wooden table. He watched as Kaleb served himself a generous portion of rice and ladled the steaming broth over the top, the steam caressing his tanned face.

"Perhaps," Kaleb agreed, catching Quon's gaze. "But silence can never teach you of the world beyond these walls. Not like words can."

"Words can be distractions," Quon countered softly, unsure if he spoke more to Kaleb or to himself. He filled his own bowl with care, each movement practiced and deliberate. The warmth of the food seeped into his fingers, comforting yet somehow disquieting.

"Distractions, or perhaps reminders that we're alive," Kaleb said, settling across from Quon with a satisfied sigh. He nodded toward Quon's bowl. "Eat up, before it gets cold. You'll need your strength if you want to keep pace with me tomorrow."

Quon chuckled despite the lingering unease. "You're right. Let's enjoy this moment for what it is." He lifted his chopsticks, savoring the first bite as the flavors exploded softly on his palate, the rice a perfect complement to the robustness of the broth.

With the savory aroma of the evening meal still lingering in the air, Kaleb animatedly shared tales of his homeland, his voice a vibrant thread weaving through the fabric of the dining hall. Quon listened with a smile, watching as Kaleb's hands painted pictures in the air, his gestures broad and full of life.

"…and you should've seen the size of the birds there!" Kaleb exclaimed, stretching his arms wide. "Their wings would blot out the sun as they passed overhead."

The table erupted with laughter, echoes of mirth mingling with the clinking of chopsticks against bowls. Hakana leaned forward, his eyes alight with curiosity. "Surely you exaggerate, Kaleb. Birds as large as clouds?"

Kaleb winked, a playful glint in his eye. "Perhaps I do, but only slightly. The world beyond these walls is vast and full of wonders."

Quon chuckled, his heart lightened by the camaraderie. He lifted a bite of rice to his mouth, savoring the textures and flavors, allowing himself to be momentarily transported by Kaleb's stories to distant lands where the mundane did not exist.

As Kaleb launched into another anecdote, an elder monk approached, his saffron robe whispering against the stone floor. The man's aged face was serene, yet his eyes bore the weight of years spent in silent contemplation.

"Kaleb," the monk said, his voice low but carrying the strength of flowing water. "You would be wise to save your energy for the food in front of you, rather than exhausting it through your incessant chatter."

A hush fell over the group as they turned their attention to the elder, whose presence commanded respect. Kaleb paused mid-gesture, a sheepish grin spreading across his face. "Of course, master. My apologies if my tales have been a distraction."

Quon watched as the monk nodded, his gaze lingering on Kaleb for a moment longer before he continued on his way. The silence that followed was profound, filled with unspoken words and the soft sounds of eating.

The night air was thick with the hum of cicadas, a rhythmic cacophony that seemed to vibrate through the walls of the dining hall. The sound crescendoed, seeping into the sanctuary of candlelit tranquility, reminding Quon and his companions of the world beyond their secluded abode.

Quon's hand paused, his chopsticks halfway to his mouth as the shrill chorus pierced the silence of the room, each chirp a needle pricking at the edges of his consciousness. He glanced up momentarily, catching Hakana's eye across the table and offering a wry smile, an unspoken acknowledgment of nature's persistent call.

"Sounds like they're singing for us tonight," Hakana remarked, his voice barely rising above the din as he gestured towards the open window with his own pair of chopsticks.

"Or perhaps they're warning us," Quon replied, the words slipping out before he could catch them, tinged with an inexplicable edge.

"Warning? You're starting to sound like elder Zhen during his ominous prophecies," Hakana chuckled, shaking his head while turning his attention back to his meal.

Quon returned his gaze to the bowl in front of him, the warm steam wafting up to mingle with the cooler air. But as he looked down, a sudden chill descended upon him, forcing his breath to hitch in his throat. His eyes widened, staring not at the nourishing food he had been about to savor but at something that sent dread coursing through his veins.

His companion's laughter sounded distant now, drowned out by the pounding pulse in his ears. His fingers trembled, the smooth wood of the chopsticks suddenly alien and cumbersome in his grasp. A slick sheen of sweat formed on his brow, beading and trickling down his temple as he continued to stare, paralyzed by the sight.

Quon's breath caught in his throat, the clamor of cicadas fading to a distant hum as he fixated on the grotesque metamorphosis unfolding within his bowl. The grains of rice writhed, elongating into pale, segmented bodies that coiled and uncoiled with sickening fluidity. His stomach churned as the broth darkened, thickening into a viscous, blood-red sludge that clung to his chopsticks like congealed lifeblood. White morsels of meat pulsed, expanding into fleshy, bloody chunks that seemed to pulsate with an unholy rhythm.

"Quon? You've gone white as the moon," Hakana observed, his voice tinged with concern. He leaned closer, peering at the contents of Quon's bowl. "What is it? A bug?" The words pulled Quon's attention briefly from the abhorrent sight, his friend's innocent question echoing absurdly against the terror gripping him.

"No... no, not a bug," Quon whispered, the words barely escaping his lips. His gaze was drawn back to the bowl, unable to escape the nightmare before him.

"Then what's wrong?" Hakana pressed, his eyebrows knitting together in confusion. The normalcy of his tone, so at odds with the horror in Quon's vision, made the scene all the more surreal.

47

Quon tried to respond, to articulate the chaos swirling in his mind, but found himself unable to form coherent thoughts. Instead, his hand trembled, sending a single drop of the red sludge splattering onto the table, its sound magnified in his ears. It was real, wasn't it? It had to be.

The voices around them continued unabated, a symphony of laughter and conversation that now felt foreign to Quon's ears. How could they not see? How could they not feel the dread that filled him, as if the very air were thick with malevolence?

With effort, he tore his eyes away from the bowl, seeking solace in Hakana's steady presence. But the panic that latched onto his heart refused to unclench, and Quon found himself gasping for air, each breath a battle against the weight pressing down on his chest.

"Something's not right," Quon finally managed to choke out, his voice a shadow of its usual strength. "I can't..." His words trailed off as he fought to maintain control, to keep the creeping darkness at bay.

Hakana reached over, placing a reassuring hand on Quon's shoulder. "It's just food, Quon. See?" He gestured towards his own bowl, identical to Quon's save for the absence of macabre transformations.

But Quon couldn't shake the image, the feeling of wrongness that pervaded his senses. This was no simple trick of the light, or a fleeting shadow born from fatigue. Something deeper, more sinister, lurked within his mind—or perhaps beyond it.

"Maybe you need rest," Jade suggested, misinterpreting Quon's silence for exhaustion. "You've pushed yourself hard today."

"Rest," Quon repeated, the word hollow as he pondered its meaning. Could sleep offer sanctuary from what he'd seen? Or would the darkness follow him even into his dreams? He didn't know, and that uncertainty frayed the edges of his resolve.

"Go on," Hakana urged gently, giving Quon's shoulder a squeeze. "We'll clean up here."

Nodding numbly, Quon rose from his seat, each movement sluggish, as if he were wading through a dense fog. He left the dining hall behind, stepping into the night where the relentless chorus of cicadas awaited him, indifferent to the turmoil that shook his soul.

"Geesh," Kaleb's voice rolled after him, tinged with his customary dry wit, "must have been a large bug."

Outside, the cool air did little to soothe Quon's fevered brow. With each hurried step, his sandals slapped the pathway stones, a staccato accompaniment to his racing thoughts. Was it exhaustion? The relentless training, the unyielding discipline—it demanded everything. Perhaps he had finally cracked, the pressure splintering his mind like brittle wood.

"Get it together," he muttered under his breath, trying to anchor himself to reality. But the shadows between the trees seemed to dance mockingly, whispering doubts with every rustling leaf.

His reflection in the koi pond caught his eye—a distorted image rippling with every anxious tremor that coursed through him. This wasn't him. This couldn't be him. The calm, centered disciple had vanished, replaced by this... apparition of fear.

"Focus, Quon," he whispered to his own wavering image. "Remember Sifu's teachings."

Inhale. Hold. Exhale. He attempted the measured breathing that Sifu had instilled in them, but each breath came too fast, too shallow.

"Quon..."

Quon's fingers wrapped around the hilt of his sword, a cold sweat beading at his brow. The reassuring solidity of the weapon under his grasp was the only anchor he had to the reality he knew.

The voice sliced through the tension, a familiar timbre that coaxed his tight muscles to relax ever so slightly. Yet, his grip on the sword did not wane, nor did the sense of being watched subside. He remained frozen, caught between relief and residual panic, waiting for the owner of the voice to step forward from the shroud of night.

"No need for that, my son," Sifu said calmly. His silhouette emerged from the shadows, the moonlight casting an ethereal glow upon his weathered features.

"Master?" Quon's voice cracked, betraying his inner turmoil. How had Sifu managed to approach undetected? Could the master be the source of his unease, or was the presence he felt something else entirely?

"Your mind is a storm, young disciple," came the knowing reply. "You must calm the winds before they uproot you."

Quon's breath hitched, the steel in his hand now feeling foreign, heavy. Slowly, he allowed the tip of the blade to kiss the ground, his arm trembling from the weight of his dread.

"Master..." he started, but words failed him, falling away into the abyss of his anxiety.

"Come," Sifu beckoned, stepping into the moonlight at last. "We have much to discuss."

"Am I going mad?" Quon couldn't keep the quiver from his voice as he followed, his sword now

sheathed but his hand remaining by its side—
comfort in familiarity, comfort in steel.

"Madness is but a step on the path," Sifu mused
cryptically. "One that can lead back to wisdom if
tread carefully."

"Or off the cliff into the abyss," Quon added
quietly, casting a final glance over his shoulder at
the garden that once promised peace but now
whispered secrets he felt he would never
understand.

"Come," Sifu beckoned, his aged hand motioning
towards a path shrouded in twilight shadows. "Let
us go visit Kijo the healer."

Quon's steps were hesitant as he followed, a disciple
trailing behind his mentor. His thoughts churned
with unease at what the shaman might reveal. Was
his dedication faltering? Did his resolve lack the
purity required by their sacred arts?

He could almost hear the distant thrumming of the
gong that had welcomed the dawn, a reminder of
the cyclical nature of existence. Life, training,
trials—they were all part of an eternal pattern. Yet,
where did Quon fit within this tapestry? Was he
merely a thread destined to fray and break?

As they approached the healer's quarters, the scent
of medicinal herbs wafted through the air, mingling
with the underlying fragrance of incense. It was a

scent that spoke of healing and age-old wisdom, a scent that had comforted many before him.

"Kijo has helped many before you," Sifu said quietly, sensing the trepidation that gripped his pupil. "Trust in her knowledge, as you trust in the teachings of our temple."

Quon nodded, steeling himself for the encounter. He would face this challenge as he had faced all others: head-on, with the determination that had been instilled in him since his first day within these hallowed grounds.

Kijo appeared in the doorway, her frame small but formidable against the backdrop of her sanctuary filled with mystic charm. "Come, child," she called out, her voice carrying the weight of years spent in service to healing.

The healer's hut was a cradle of ancient wisdom, its walls lined with shelves of herbs and roots that held secrets of the old ways. A hint of incense lingered in the air, mingling with the earthy aroma of dried plants. Quon stood in the center of this sanctum, feeling as if the very air were steeped in quietude.

"It seems you have been experiencing some hallucinations," the healer stated, her voice as soothing as the melody of a gently flowing stream. She peered into his eyes with a gaze that seemed to reach into the depths of his soul.

Quon's throat tightened, the words catching like leaves in a swift current. "Yes, I...I have," he admitted, the shadows of his ordeal flickering across his face. His hands fidgeted at his sides, betraying the turmoil within.

"Have you been under a lot of stress lately?" Her question was soft but probing, like a key turning in a lock long rusted shut.

He nodded, the motion releasing the lump that had formed in his throat, allowing the truth to spill forth. "I've been pushing myself," he confessed, his gaze dropping to where his fingers anxiously twisted the hem of his tunic. "Harder than ever before."

"Both physically and mentally," Sifu added from where he stood by the doorway, his presence an anchor in the storm of Quon's thoughts.

Quon's mind raced back over unending days of rigorous training, his relentless drive to excel, to meet the expectations that seemed etched into the very stones of the temple. He could almost feel the weight of each bruise, the echo of labored breaths, the sting of sweat in his eyes—all markers of his journey toward an ideal that felt increasingly elusive.

"Sometimes, we forget that strength also needs rest," the healer continued, her hand reaching out to still his restless fingers. Her touch was warm, grounding, a reminder of the physical world when his mind threatened to spiral once again into chaos.

In the silence that followed, punctuated only by the soft crackle of the oil lamp, Quon wrestled with the realization that had crept upon him like the slow unfurling of dawn. He had been teetering on the edge, dancing with shadows born from his own fervor.

"Your determination is commendable," Sifu said, stepping closer. "But even the sharpest blade must be sheathed to preserve its edge."

The words settled over Quon like a mantle, heavy with truth. He exhaled slowly, letting go of the tension that had become his constant companion. In the dim light of the hut, he felt the boundaries of his body, the cadence of his pulse—a drumbeat of life that demanded respect for its limitations.

"Your path is not a sprint, but a marathon," the healer murmured, drawing Quon's attention back to her wise, weathered face. "You must allow yourself moments of stillness amidst the striving."

Quon closed his eyes, allowing her wisdom to seep into his bones. When he opened them again, the world seemed less daunting, the specters of his fears less potent. He was ready to listen, to learn, and to heal.

Kijo's fingers traced the raised scar of the emblem on Quon's chest, a brand that signified his belonging to the temple. The symbol, an intricate knotwork dragon coiling around a blossoming lotus, seemed to pulse with his quickening heartbeat. He remembered the pride he felt when the searing pain of the iron had etched his commitment into his flesh. But now, that same mark throbbed with a foreboding reminder of the covenant he feared he might break.

"Many have sat where you now sit," the healer, Kijo, spoke as her hands hovered over his tense shoulders. Her voice was a balm, her words carrying the weight of ancient wisdom passed down through generations. "The path demands much, and not all who walk it can endure."

Her touch was light, almost ethereal, as if she could smooth away the creases of his troubled thoughts with the gentlest caress. Quon inhaled sharply, the air heavy with the scent of medicinal herbs and smoke from the incense burning in the corner of the hut.

"Will I be sent away like the others?" he whispered, the question slipping out like the quietest confession, his gaze fixed on the dirt floor, where shadows danced with the flicker of candlelight.

"Focus on my voice," Kijo instructed, her palm warm against his cool forehead. "Let go of the 'what ifs.' Be here, now, with me."

As Kijo began to hum, a simple melody that filled the small space with an aura of tranquility, Quon allowed his eyelids to fall shut. The persistent hammering of his heart slowed, beat by measured beat, syncing with the rhythm of the tune. The warmth from her hand bled into him, spreading like sunlight on a winter's morning—gentle yet pervasive.

His mind painted images of the temple grounds—the cherry blossoms in bloom, the stone pathways warmed by the sun, the laughter of his fellow disciples. A surge of emotion welled up within him, a mingling of love for this place and a visceral fear of losing it all.

"Your spirit is strong, but it must not shackle you," Kijo said, breaking the silence that cocooned them. "You are more than your fears, Quon. More than this moment of doubt."

"Sometimes, I feel like I am drowning," Quon admitted, his voice barely above a murmur, betraying his vulnerability. "As if the very air I breathe is water, and I cannot find the surface."

"Remember, even the greatest sea has both ebbs and flows," she replied, her thumb drawing soothing circles on his temple. "You must ride the waves, not fight them."

Quon exhaled, a long and deliberate breath, envisioning the tension within him unraveling, unspooling into the ether. Kijo's song continued, notes hanging in the air, each one cradling his spirit, lifting the heaviness that had settled upon his chest.

The world beyond his closed eyes ceased to exist, replaced by an inner sanctum where only peace reigned. With each passing second, the grip of his anxieties loosened, his muscles relinquishing their coiled readiness. In the depth of his surrender, Quon found an unexpected comfort, an acceptance of his own humanity.

"Let the emblem on your chest not be a chain, but a reminder of your connection to all things," Kijo whispered into his ear, her words echoing in the stillness. "We are one, you and I, and the path ahead."

"Thank you," Quon breathed out, the words a silent vow, a promise to honor the sacred bond between disciple and mentor, student and healer, body and soul.

Quon's eyelids fluttered open, the dim glow of a single oil lamp casting long shadows across the room. Sifu's aged face was etched with lines of concern, his forehead wrinkled in contemplation as he peered down at his pupil. Beside him stood Kijo, her expression a gentle blend of worry and reassurance.

"Ah, you return to us," Sifu said, a trace of relief softening his normally stern voice.

Quon propped himself up on his elbows, his head spinning slightly from the abrupt shift between worlds. The warmth that had infused his body lingered; a protective cocoon spun by Kijo's healing energy. He offered them a weak smile, a silent acknowledgment of their presence and care.

"Your spirit wandered far, young Quon," Kijo spoke tenderly, her hand remaining on his forehead as if she could anchor him to the here and now.

Quon nodded, the ghost of his harrowing vision still clawing at the edges of his mind. "I saw... things that cannot be unseen," he murmured, the tremble in his voice belying the calm he tried to project.

As Quon sat up fully, the sacred emblem seared into his skin tingled, a reminder of his commitment and the shared journey of all who wore it. With each steady breath, he felt his center returning, the chaos within receding like a storm passing over calm seas.

"Let your mind rest, child," Kijo whispered, her fingers tracing the air above his emblem, invoking an ancient blessing. "You are held by forces greater than your own doubts."

"Thank you," he breathed, the gratitude flowing from him like a river breaking its banks. His words carried the weight of a vow renewed—to honor the teachings, to trust in his mentors, and to embrace the unity etched into his very flesh.

With the guidance of his teacher and the care of the healer, Quon lay back down, his body sinking into the straw mat beneath him. His eyelids grew heavy, the world softening around him as he surrendered to the pull of sleep.

CHAPTER 3
A CURSED AWAKENING

The resounding toll of the gong sliced through the morning stillness, a resonant cadence that seemed to stir the very soul of the temple. Each vibration cascaded against the time-worn stone, a primal awakening that caused the air itself to shiver with reverence. Amidst this orchestral symphony, a chorus of birds added their lilting melodies while the rhythmic clack-clack of bamboo swords resounded, punctuating the dawn with the sound of discipline and precision.

The tranquil stream that cut across the courtyard caught the burgeoning daylight, its waters turning from a pensive gray to a liquid tapestry of shimmering golds and silvers. It was a moment of beauty so stark it nearly snatched Quon's attention away from the duel at hand, but he steadied himself, channeling the tranquility of the scene into his next move.

Quon's feet moved with purpose, each step on the cold stone floor a testament to his commitment. His hands deftly wielded the wooden sword, a seamless extension of his will. The temple air was copious with concentration, the scent of incense and the sound of exertion melding into a blend of sacred tradition.

"Control," he breathed to himself, muscles tensing and relaxing in a precise rhythm, guiding Hakana through a series of complex maneuvers.

"Remember, it's not just about strength—it's about knowing when and how to use it."

"Like water," Hakana replied, his voice a low hum of focus as he matched Quon's intensity.

Hakana mirrored Quon's motions with an iron resolve etched on his features, a living embodiment of the discipline demanded by their path.

Jade, ever the picture of fluidity, flowed from stance to stance, her technique painting strokes of artistry in the air. Her eyes were half-closed, as if she could see beneath the surface of the movements to the deeper meaning they held.

Kaleb, meanwhile, lingered on the periphery of this representation of dedication. He watched with a crooked grin, unable to mirror the solemnity that came so naturally to his companions.

"Anyone ever tell you three that you're way too serious?" Kaleb jested, disrupting the harmony with a chuckle. He swung his sword lazily, more performer than pupil, delighting in the simple pleasure of movement.

"Kaleb!" Quon's voice cut through the laughter like a blade. "This is no laughing matter. These techniques have been honed over centuries. Respect them."

"Ah, come on, Quon. You can't tell me you don't feel the thrill of this?" Kaleb retorted, spinning his weapon with a flourish that was all showmanship and no substance. The temple walls seemed to frown upon him, the weight of ancient eyes pressing down.

"Thrill? Yes. But there is also reverence," Quon countered, pausing to lock eyes with Kaleb, willing him to understand. "We are walking a path paved by the sacrifices of many."

"Maybe I'm just paving my own way," Kaleb exclaimed aloud, his smile faltering for a moment as he considered his place among these stone-faced sentinels of tradition.

"Your way?" Hakana interjected, his tone sharp as a fresh whetstone. "Is that what you call disregarding the importance of our training?"

"Perhaps your 'way' is why you stumble where we find footing," Jade added, the disappointment clear in her otherwise serene expression.

Kaleb's carefree mask slipped further, revealing a flicker of doubt. Was he truly out of step with the dance of the samurai? Or was he simply hearing a different tune, one less rigid and defined?

Kaleb sighed, shaking his head with a rueful laugh. He took up his position once more, trying to mimic the focus of his peers.

The ancient wooden floor of the dojo groaned softly underfoot as Kaleb executed a series of lethargic cuts, his bamboo sword swishing through air with less vigor than the breeze outside. A bead of sweat meandered down his brow, tracing the contours of his face before plummeting to the ground, ignored like the discipline he was expected to uphold.

"Kaleb," came a stern voice from the shadows, and the assembled trainees stiffened, their practice halting as they turned towards the source. The eldest of the temple guardians stepped into the light, his eyes like flint striking sparks against Kaleb's casual defiance.

"Your blade weaves a tale," the elder said, "but it speaks not of honor or dedication. It whispers of shortcuts, of a journey half-walked."

Kaleb attempted a sheepish grin, hoping to deflect the gravity of the moment. "Maybe my story's just getting started, you know? Every hero stumble at first."

The silence that followed was suffocating, each second stretching longer than the last. The other elders emerged beside their companion, forming a tribunal of wisdom and judgment. Their faces were etched with concern, their gazes unwavering as they beheld the wayward pupil.

"Kaleb," another elder began, his voice resonating through the quiet dojo, "the path of the samurai is strewn with trials that shape the spirit. To neglect these is to wander lost in the fog of dishonor."

Around him, his fellow acolytes stood motionless, their eyes darting between him and the elders, uncertain of which held more weight—their sympathy for a friend or their reverence for tradition.

Kaleb felt the weight of their stares like the oppressive humidity that preceded a storm. His throat tightened, the jovial retort he had ready now clinging desperately to his lips, unspoken. He knew their respect for the elders ran deep—deeper, perhaps, than their camaraderie with him.

His mind spun, seeking an escape but finding none. He wanted to laugh, to break the tension with a quip, but the somber faces before him held no room for levity. In the pit of his stomach, a knot tightened—one woven from threads of guilt and the dawning recognition of his own failings.

"Training ends not when the gong echoes its final note," the third elder added solemnly, "but when the heart and soul have embraced the discipline fully. Have yours, Kaleb?"

The elders' words sunk into him, heavy and cold. They echoed off the walls, reverberating like a drumbeat of impending consequence. Kaleb swallowed hard, feeling the fortress of his carefree demeanor begin to crumble, stone by stone.

"Discipline... commitment... I understand they matter," Kaleb muttered, his voice barely carrying, betraying a vulnerability he seldom showed. "But doesn't the heart need freedom to truly commit?"

"Freedom without purpose is a leaf adrift on the wind," the first elder replied. "Purposeful freedom is the leaf that chooses its path downstream."

Kaleb's gaze dropped to the sword in his hand, seeing it not as an extension of his will, but as a symbol of what he was yet to grasp. In the silence that followed.

A flock of birds erupted from the nearby trees abruptly breaking the silence, their cries punctuating the solemnity of the moment. Kaleb's hands tightened into fists at his sides, fingernails digging into his palms. He could no longer hide behind his charm; the gravity of his situation pressed down upon him like the weight of the mountain under which the temple stood.

"Forgive me, elders," Kaleb began, his voice strained as he grappled with the words. "I admit, I've been... distracted."

His plea hung in the air, vulnerable and raw. He searched their faces for a sign of understanding, a flicker of leniency.

"I need more guidance," he implored, desperation seeping into his tone. "More assistance. If I am to become a true samurai, I must learn how to balance the rigors of training with the... the majesty that surrounds us."

But the elders remained as immovable as the ancient rocks that lined the temple's foundation. Their expression did not waver, their resolve as firm as the traditions they upheld.

"Distractions are but tests of focus," the second elder said, his voice echoing off the stone walls. "One does not become a true samurai by succumbing to them."

Kaleb's throat constricted. He knew their words were just, yet his heart rebelled against the notion of such stringent control. His eyes dropped to his feet.

The words struck Kaleb like arrows, each one piercing deeper than the last. He could see the resolve in the elders' ancient eyes, the decision irrevocably made. His breath hitched, caught between the duty he owed to himself and the loyalty he felt toward those who had stood by him.

"Please," Kaleb implored, his voice strained with the sincerity of his plea, "let me try again. I know I can embrace the discipline you speak of."

But the silence that followed was his answer, a void that no promise could fill. Jade's tears finally breached their banks, cascading down her cheeks even as she stood dignified and strong.

"Your path diverges from ours now," the first elder stated, his voice final, severing the last thread of hope.

The command resonated in Kaleb's chest, a hollow echo that marked the end of his tenure within these sacred walls.

Quon's arms, as sturdy as the ancient oaks that flanked the temple's entrance, wrapped around Kaleb in a desperate grip. Hakana and Jade joined the embrace, their bodies forming a shield against the inevitability of farewell. The stillness of the dawn was punctuated only by the sound of their mingled breaths, heavy with unspoken grief.

"Remember us," Jade's voice was a whisper against Kaleb's ear, her words piercing the silence like the first drops of rain on parched earth.

"Always," Kaleb choked out, his eyes stinging as he clung to her and the others. His mind raced, replaying every shared laughter and lesson, each moment now a shard of memory too painful to hold yet impossible to release.

Hakana, normally the quietest among them, found strength in his sorrow, "This is not the end of your journey, brother. You carry us with you, as we keep a part of you here."

Kaleb's heart swelled at the conviction in Hakana's tone, an ache forming where gratitude and loss intertwined. He nodded, unable to trust his voice, feeling the raw edges of a future without these familiar souls by his side.

Quon released him last, stepping back with a solemn nod. "In another life, perhaps our paths will converge once more. Until then, walk with honor, Kaleb."

"Without discipline, what am I?" Kaleb asked, half-rhetorical, his gaze flitting between the faces of his closest companions. "But I'll find my way. For all of you."

They stepped away from each other, the physical distance echoing the emotional chasm that yawned open with each passing second. Quon began reciting the words of parting from the ancient texts, a ritual meant to grant safe passage to those who leave the temple's fold. The others joined in, three voices blending into a melancholic cadence that seemed to vibrate within the very air around them.

"May the winds be ever at your back, and the sun shine warm upon your face..."

"May the rains fall soft upon your fields, and until we meet again..."

"May you be held in the palm of enlightenment."

The finality of the ritual weighed heavily upon them, a somber cloud that eclipsed the golden rays of morning. Kaleb bowed deeply, his respect for the traditions and those he left behind evident in the deference of his posture.

With that, he turned following the elders into the temple, his silhouette cutting a stark figure against the lightening sky. The temple bells tolled once more, their resonance a haunting accompaniment to the sight of Kaleb's departure. Quon, Hakana, and Jade watched until he became a mere speck in the distance, their hearts laden with a sorrow that only time could hope to ease.

The silence was impenetrable, each breath a palpable entity in the charged air. Quon's gaze never wavered as the elders, robes whispering against the stone floor, guided Kaleb through the great wooden doors of the temple. Hakana's hand found his shoulder, a silent anchor amid the storm of emotions churning within him. Beside them, Jade's eyes shimmered with unshed tears, her lips moving in a silent prayer for their friend.

"Look," Hakana murmured, a note of awe threading his voice as Sifu materialized like a wraith from the morning mist, his presence commanding even in its subtlety.

With a candle in hand, Sifu's silhouette was etched against the backdrop of dawn's light. "Do you now see the true weight of why it's imperative to stay dedicated to your path?" The master questioned; his voice soft yet laden with an ancient wisdom that burrowed deep into Quon's core.

"We let this candle burn as a reminder," he whispered, his voice so soft it seemed to blend with the silence of the chamber. "A reminder of the consequences that befall those who do not show respect to our ancient customs and traditions."

Quon nodded once, solemnly, his throat tight as he watched Sifu lower himself gracefully to place the candle beside others already flickering with a quiet resolve. The tiny flames seemed to hold the collective memories and lessons of the temple within their dance.

"To stray is to lose oneself," Sifu added, his voice, echoing the gravity of his words.

Sifu straightened, fixating on each of them with a piercing stare that seemed to reach into their very souls. "Kaleb has chosen his path, now you must continue to forge yours with even greater conviction."

Quon could feel the weight of responsibility settling on his shoulders, heavier than the bamboo sword he wielded every day. He glanced at Hakana, whose determination was mirrored in the set of his jaw, and then to Jade, who despite her grief, stood resolute and unwavering.

The trio bowed in respect as their master disappears into the hallway of the temple. As they turned to leave, Quon, Hakana, and Jade share one last look at the burning candles now understanding the meaning of their presence throughout all the temple's grounds. With heavy hearts, they proceeded back to training, their minds focused on the challenges that lay ahead and the memory of their departed friend.

CHAPTER 4
PUPPETRY OF THE GNOK ARMY

The silvery disc of the moon bathed the sprawling temple in an otherworldly light. Its pale beams penetrated the crevices of the ancient stonework, upon the meditating group of students, casting long, spectral shadows that seemed to stretch and beckon with ghostly fingers.

In the dim light of the moon, the figures of Quon, Hakana, and Jade could barely be made out as they crept away from the group. Their movements were quick and silent, gliding through the shadows with ease not to disturb the mediating student nor the elders.

The three figures, cloaked in darkness, meet in the shadows cast by the moon. Their silhouettes blend, almost indistinguishable from one another.

"Have you noticed the way the moonlight never seems to touch the eastern wall?" Quon whispered, his gaze locked on the part of the temple that remained stubbornly enshrouded in darkness.

Jade, standing beside them, pulled her cloak tighter around her shoulders. "It's as if the light is afraid to reveal what's hidden there," she murmured, a hint of fear lacing her voice.

Hakana nodded slowly, his mind racing with the strange occurrences they had all witnessed since their arrival. The echoes of disembodied whispers that seemed to emanate from the walls, the fleeting glimpses of shadows where none should be – all these things had once been easy to dismiss. But now...

"Sometimes, I hear the stones weeping at night," Quon said, his voice barely above a breath. "As though the temple itself mourns something lost—or fears something coming."

"Can a place have a memory?" Hakana pondered aloud, his logical mind grappling with the idea. "A consciousness that remembers its past?"

"Or maybe it's a warning," Jade added, her eyes scanning the darkness for any sign of movement.

Their shared experiences had bound them together, their bond forged in the ambiguity of their sanctuary. It was here, among the scrolls and the sparring, that they had found purpose. Yet, as the years passed, so too did the veneer of safety begin to crack, revealing unsettling truths beneath.

"Remember when Master Chen told us that every stone in this temple has been laid with intention, with a story to tell?" Quon turned to face his friends, searching their faces for understanding.

"Yes, but those stories were supposed to be about harmony and balance, not... whatever this is," Hakana said, gesturing vaguely at the oppressive atmosphere that enveloped them.

"Perhaps the stories changed," Jade suggested, her eyes distant. "Or perhaps there are chapters we were never meant to read."

They huddled closer, their whispers blending with the soft rustle of leaves in the gentle wind. In the safety of their closeness, they allowed themselves a moment of vulnerability, sharing their fears for their mentors—the men and women who had become their family.

"I just can't shake off this feeling of dread," Quon admitted, his hands clenched into fists at his sides. "Like we're on the cusp of something dark."

"Whatever it is, we'll face it together," Hakana declared, his determination a tangible force in the uncertain night.

"Agreed. We owe it to the elders," Jade said, her resolve hardening. "They've guided us this far. We can't let them face whatever this is alone."

Nodding in silent accord, they each took solace in the unspoken oath they had made to one another. As the moon continued its slow ascent, the companions fled back to their mediation.

Later that evening, after the students had been led through a deep meditation session, Jade lingered behind under the pretense of seeking further tranquility. Her feet made soft sounds against the stone floor as she neared the elders' chambers. They should have been deep in their own meditative practices by now, the door closed to all outside interruption.

A flicker of movement caught her eye, and she paused—a shadow passed across the narrow slit of light beneath the door. Curiosity piqued, Jade pressed her ear to the cool wood, listening for the familiar pulse of joint reflection.

Jade put her hands on each side of the door slowly bringing her head closer. She then peaked through the keyhole, the sight that met her eyes was one of grotesque ritual: the elders, their bodies rooted like ancient trees, formed a perfect circle within the chamber. Their heads, however, were anything but still, jerking side to side with an eerie rhythm that defied the natural order of their physical forms. It was as if they were marionettes, their strings yanked by unseen hands.

A slithering fear coiled in her gut, its icy grip tightening with each contorted grimace that flashed across the elders' faces.

"Is this what becomes of us?" Jade pondered, dread seeping into the marrow of her bones. "Is this the end result of our training?"

The flicker of candlelight lent an otherworldly aura to the scene. Shadows cavorted on the walls, giving form to the horror that gripped Jade's psyche. The air itself seemed concentrated with something unspeakable, a malignant presence that danced just beyond the realm of sight.

"Focus," she instructed herself, fighting the urge to flee. "Remember Quon's visions. There is a connection here."

Her gaze locked onto the nearest elder, Master Lin, whose features twisted into expressions of anguish then glee, cycling through emotions as if sampling them for the first time. His mouth moved rapidly, shaping words—or perhaps incantations—that were lost in the cacophony of disjointed murmurs filling the room.

A shiver coursed down her backbone, the kind that whispered of forbidden knowledge and spectral hauntings. This was not the serene meditation she'd grown accustomed to; this was a descent into madness, a ceremony that flirted with the abyss.

She retreated, her back pressed to the cold, unyielding stone of the hallway, her mind whirling with the implications of her discovery.

"Quon... Hakana... we have much to discuss," she vowed, the steel in her tone belying the tremor in her limbs. She would share everything, omitting no detail, and together they would unravel the embroidery of deceit that veiled their sacred temple.

With one last glance at the unnatural spectacle, Jade turned away, the image seared into her memory—a signal fueling her newfound purpose. They would find the truth, whatever perilous roads they must travel. She slipped away, a wraith in the darkness, her conviction unwavering.

On the other side of temple, the silent corridors twisted like the serpentine roots of an ancient tree, each turn obscured by shadow and mystique. Hakana found himself lost strolling through the vast tunnels beneath the temple. His footsteps were light upon the stone floors, his presence a mere whisper between burning candles in the vast expanse of hallowed halls.

His gaze locked on the ornate wooden door standing before him. The symbols etched into its surface— circles intertwined with lines and dots in an elaborate dance—seemed to pulse with a life of their own.

Hakana's breath came in shallow gasps, his heart drumming a frenzied beat against his ribcage as he neared the threshold of the forbidden. His shadow slipped along the cold stone floor; a silent specter drawn towards the enigmatic allure of the off-limits chamber.

"Careful, Hakana, just a peek," he counseled himself as he crept forward, his body taut with the awareness of the risk he undertook. Peering through the slender divide, a world apart from everything he had known about the temple manifested before his eyes.

The light within was alive, pulsating like the heartbeat of some ethereal beast, casting a phantasmagoria of shadows that crept and retreated across the walls. The symbols, etched with meticulous care upon the ancient stone, now appeared to dance—an infernal ballet orchestrated by forces unseen.

"Jade would say these symbols are a language," he told himself, his gaze affixed on the undulating patterns of light and darkness. "A language we have not been taught to read." The realization was a splinter in his mind, impossible to ignore.

"Four days," he breathed, retreating from the crack through which the otherworldly scene spilled forth.

"In four days, under the shroud of the new moon, we will uncover the truth." The words were a vow.

Quon, Hakana, and Jade each returned to their respective beds with the stealth of shadows sliding across the floor. A silent understanding passed between them as they slid beneath their sheets, their eyes locking for a moment in the dim light – a shared resolve that words were too crude to convey.

"Are you certain we weren't followed?" Jade's whisper cut through the thick silence like a knife, barely more than the rustle of leaves outside.

"Positive," Hakana replied, his voice equally subdued. "I doubled back twice."

"Good. Remember, normal routines tomorrow," Quon added, a soft command that hung in the air before dissipating into the night.

The trio agreed to execute their plan together in four days. The new moon would provide the least amount of light in the night's sky making it easier to hide in the shadows to finally unearth the secrets that have been longing for answers.

CHAPTER 5
DANCE OF ECHOES

The night was dark and damp, the air thick as the temple lay shrouded in silence of the night.

Quon, Hakana, and Jade found themselves in the shadows of their chamber, their silhouettes mere contours in the dim light. The eve of the mission was upon them, and the weight of the unknown bore heavily on Quon's shoulders. He felt a profound sense of responsibility and concern for his friends.

"Hakana, Jade," Quon began, his voice laced with both love and worry, "I've been thinking. This mission is unlike anything we've faced before. The risks are high, and if we were to be caught, I'm willing to bear the consequences. But I wouldn't be able to live with myself of the thought of both of you being banished from the temple."

Hakana and Jade exchanged glances, understanding the depth of Quon's concern. However, they weren't willing to back down without expressing their own convictions.

Hakana spoke first, his voice firm but compassionate. "Quon, we appreciate your worry, and it comes from a place of love and friendship. But we've trained together, shared in every battle, and faced countless hardships as a team. We can't let fear dictate our choices now. We need to stand together."

Jade, just as determined, declared, "If there is something truly terrible happening, we might be able to put a stop to it, protecting ourselves and saving Sifu and the elder monks."

Quon looked from Hakana to Jade, a mixture of gratitude and anxiety in his eyes. "I can't help but worry, but if you're determined to come, then promise me you'll stay close, and we'll watch out for each other."

Hakana and Jade nodded in agreement, their unwavering determination a testament to their strong bond and their shared commitment to each other.

The night slowly rolled by, and the trio eventually concluded their outing. Feeling exhausted, they head toward their mats.

Quon waited patiently, his body loose and relaxed as if he was sleeping. His heartbeat fast with anxiety but his breathing was shallow and slow.

When all had been silent for some time, Quon finally moved. The prospect stealthily stands up and pads away barefoot with the grace of a swift ninja vanishing into the shadows.

He silently snuck out of his sleeping quarters, not wanting to wake or alarm anyone else with his movements. He always kept one hand on his weapon as he carefully navigated through the dark corridors of the temple and made his way towards its inner sanctum.

His heartbeat loudly in his ears like a drum, drowning out any other sound around him. His breathing was shallow and quick as if he was trying to keep it as quiet as possible. There was a feeling of electricity in the air, an energy full of anticipation and unease that seemed to stop at the threshold of the door.

Finally arriving the large oak door that marked the entrance of the inner chamber, Quon was careful as he manipulated the lock with his self-made picklock. After a few quick clicks, the door unlocks. Quon opened it slowly and stepped inside, allowing his eyes time to adjust to its darkness as he scanned for any sign of life or potential danger lurking around.

To Quon's surprise, all seemed peaceful - no one present in sight - yet still something felt off about this place; an unspoken energy so heavy you could taste it in the air as if unseen forces were watching him from afar with trepidation and anticipation.

He remembered what Hakana had said about how they should trust their gut intuition when entering unknown situations such as this one; so, trusting that instinct now, Quon traversed further into the chamber in search for answers despite every nerve in his body telling him otherwise.

He needed to know what was going on, what secrets the elders were potentially hiding from them.

Deeper inside the massive chamber, he comes across an area filled with ancient artifacts and satanic symbols all over the walls and floor. Candles illuminating the ground of the dark area. He sees runes inscribed in the stone walls, intricate talismans hanging from the ceiling, and old books scattered around, their pages adorned with unknown symbols.

The center of the room stood a stone pedestal, upon which rested a glowing crystal. Quon approached it cautiously, feeling drawn to its light. As he got closer, he realized that the crystal was emitting a low hum, almost like a warning.

Quon extended his arms, sweat dripping from his forehead as he reached for the stone and wrapped his fingers around the pulsating relic. The artifact hummed in his grip, vibrating with an intensity that threatened to jolt his body with its sheer force.

His hands were sliced open by the object's sharp edges, bleeding onto the stone base as he struggled against its magnetic force. The glowing, mysterious item was a deep purple and red, crafted from materials never seen before on the planet.

With one last shudder, the artifact was free. Suddenly, the walls of the chamber began to shake, and dust rained down from the ceiling. Quon stumbled backwards, fear gripping his heart. Suddenly the mask that had been a false veil to the grand temple shattered, then begins to reveal it's true sinister appearance.

Everywhere he looked things were changing; walls crumbled before his eyes and the stones seemed to age in an instant. The temple that he thought he knew so well turned out to be a mere illusion—it was not a place of peace, but rather a cruel fortress home to the wicked Ngok Army.

Screams were heard in the distance. Everyone else that had been blinded by the curse were now seeing a new world around them. The elder monks they knew and came to love transformed into their true self, Satanic demons.

Quon stumbled backwards, his heart racing as he tried to come to grips with what he was seeing. He couldn't believe what he was seeing. His mind struggled to process the sudden realization that his entire life had been a lie.

The air was compact with the stench of sulfur and brimstone, and he could hear screams and moans echoing through the halls. Quon could hear fellow prisoner's fighting for their lives above.

As his environment began to settle into its demonic decayed form, Quon knew he had to get out of there. He turned to run but was suddenly surrounded by a group of demons. They blocked his path, snarling and began to close in on him. Panic set in as he realized he was trapped with no way out.

The demons started to laugh, their twisted faces contorting into an expression of delight at seeing him in such a vulnerable state. One of them, a towering figure with satanic marking all over his head and body, stepped forward and spoke in a deep, menacing voice.

"Hello, Quon," the demon said. "Once you were blind, and now you see." Sifu stood before him in all his monstrous glory. His towering figure was marked with symbols of evil, and his eyes were solid white, it felt like looking into the void of terror. With each step he took, the ground trembled with a force unseen before.

The words sent chills down Quon's spine as he stared up at the towering demon. He knew that he was in grave danger and had to find a way to escape. He barely had the courage to face this vile creature, whose once kind visage as his teacher, and even as a father figure now wore expression of pure evil. He could feel every muscle in his body tensing up as he fought the fear threatening to overwhelm him.

Quon's bleeding hand grips his sword as he lunged forward but was quickly parried by Sifu. Sifu swipes swiftly blocking Quon's attack. The large creature forced his blade through his pupil's side.

Quon screams before he stumbles in pain and surprise. Fighting for his life. He pushes the beast to the side then rushes towards the exit.

He could hear their enraged screams behind him as he fled, their claws scraping against the stone floor.

Finally, holding his wounded side, blood dripping to the ground as he burst through the door and into the night air. The stars were still shining, but they no longer seemed friendly. They were a reminder of the world he had left behind, a world that was now forever changed.

His eyes darted around the area, catching a glimpse of something that made his blood run cold - his fallen comrades, their bodies shredded and dismembered in grotesque pieces, with a katana still tightly grasped in their hand.

In the momentary silence he heard demons cackling in the distance, taunting him with malicious glee. Quon picked the katana up and held it tightly in his hands, his fingers trembling as he clutched both blades. He knew that if he wanted to survive this night he would need to fight back against these creatures of darkness.

The night sky lit up with flashes of lightening as Quon fought off demon after demon, wielding the katanas with strength and skill honed from years of training. He spun around them in circles, dodging their vicious attacks while slashing at them with fierce precision.

The blood of his enemies flew around him like a crimson rain while screams of agony pierced through the air. While there seemed to be no end to these demons, Quon kept on searching for his friends.

Quon creeps into one of the chambers in the temple, only to find a gruesome scene of horror. Everywhere he looks, fear-filled eyes meet his probing gaze as the unfortunate souls whom he thought had been driven away from the temple due to their inability to survive its rigorous training, now hang limply from sharp hooks suspended over a sea of crimson blood, their cries muffled by cloth gags. The helpless victims are now no more than playthings for the nightmarish creatures that roam within these cursed walls and food to the imprisoned.

Scanning the area of the tortured, his eyes pause on a familiar face, Kaleb. Kaleb was hanging in pain with missing limbs; muffled screams came from his gag and tears poured from his eyes. The wails and screams of those undergoing unspeakable torture in the distance fill the air with an abysmal dread.

Quon trudged on, fear gripping his heart with every step. He felt time running out. The group of prisoners fighting at his side was slowly dwindling as they were cut down by the monsters' vile blades. He pushed himself to fight harder, faster—a true master now in the art of swordsmanship.

Fiercely did they battle for freedom, clashing steel against steel with a unified goal: survival.

Quon's heart pounded in his chest as he watched the two companion warriors fighting against the demonic creatures. He could feel their desperation and courage radiating from them, and he wanted desperately to help. But there were too many of them, and it seemed hopeless.

Just as he was about to join the fray, a sudden force knocked him off his feet as his head slammed into the side of the stone wall. He hit the wall with a sickening thud and slumped to the ground, his vision swimming. The loud clang of his katanas hitting the ground reverberating.

As he struggled to regain his senses, Quon felt a presence at his back. He turned just in time to see a massive demon, Sifu mutated even worse than he saw him before looming over him, its solid white eyes gleaming with malice.

The demon's lips curled into a menacing grin as it lunged forward with fierce intent. Quon narrowly avoided the strike.

With their enemies at their feet, Hakana and Jade rush to Quon's aid to fight the demon, Sifu. Hakana stood up between both of his friends, katana gripped firmly. The three timed their attacks at the demon. Immediately, it was apparent. The demon proved to be too powerful, parrying even their most advanced attacks with ease.

As if a devil of war, Sifu timed Quon missing his attack quickly grabbing him, gripping his neck tightly. Quon resisted with all his might.

Before Hakana and Jade could make their move. Using one arm, Sifu lifted Quon off his feet. Quon desperately grabbed and clawed at the demon's arm trying to resist. Bones could be heard breaking and crunching as the demon's grip closed in until Quon's body fell limp from Sifu's death grip.

Jade and Hakana let out guttural roars of sorrow as they witnessed the death of their companion. But grief had to give way to survival, and they both knew that there was no chance they would be able to defeat the beast. The two desperate warriors frantically sprint away from the monstrous beast as its maniacal laughter echoes around them. The ground trembles beneath their feet, and its deafening roar blasts through the air like an unrelenting siren, threatening to tear their world.

Jade and Hakana finally make it back to the surface escaping the chaos below. It suddenly became eerily quiet as the two walked through courtyard carefully. The courtyard was blanketed with what appeared to be snow. The escapees leaving imprints behind each step they take. Jade extends her arm opening palm. She lets the weightless material falling from the sky fall onto her open palm. She closes her palm letting her fingers run the material around. "It's ash." Jade says softly.

The two stood paralyzed as a sinister laughter encircled them, growing louder and more vicious. A deathly chill ran through their spines and their arms trembled as they held firm to the weapons in their hands. Suddenly, what used to be Kijo the healer manifested itself into something even more nightmarish than before. Wearing a pale hannya mask with wide, threatening eyes and sharp teeth that glinted in the moonlight, she seemed to emanate an aura of malicious intent.

Her body moved like a shadowy phantom, swift and invisible. She effortlessly weaved through Hakana and Jade's attack strikes. Kijo brandished her blade with the strength of a thousand warriors. With her sword slicing through anything that stood in her way.

She puts her blade through Hakana's stomach with such speed and ferocity that he dropped his weapon and held his stomach with both hands, yelling out in pain. His blood spilled onto the ground as he fell to his knees unable to withstand the force of Kijo's attack.

Jade screamed out in horror as she charged towards Kijo. Kijo then swiftly turned towards Jade, no mercy or hesitance on her face as she struck again and again and again viciously until Jade lay twitching at her feet. The blood sprayed hannya mask gleamed terrifyingly in the moonlight as Kijo let out yet another chillingly satisfied chuckle.

Hakana now on his back, squirmed backwards still holding his stomach. A smeared blood trail being left behind with every inch he squirmed backward. Kijo walked slowly toward Hakana. blood dripping from her bare feet as she walked through the puddle of Jade's blood. Hakana winced in agony as he looked on upon Jade. It was unbearable to see. Jade's lifeless eyes staring back at him, with a single tear falling down her cheek.

The courtyard was now a mausoleum of desolation, deafening in its stillness. The heavens above us receded into an abyss of despair, and the stars vanished like fireflies in their stead. Darkness encased its claws as sinister shadows encroached from all sides. In one area stood the withered bonsai tree towered with its skeletal branches bowing where once Sifu sat to tell tales of lies. The smell of iron and salt filled the air, and Hakana felt a wave of nausea as he watched the lifeless bodies of his comrades and closest people he's ever known crumpled in pools of their own blood. He could only hear the roar of the river, which ran deep and fast to its destination, cutting through the temple's courtyard. Kijo continued to stalk closer and closer, and Hakana desperately sought refuge at the edge of the water. He could feel its icy chill, yet he knew it would provide solace.

With a bust of the last bit of his energy, Hakana plunged into the river trying to escape the terror that had consumed the temple, the icy coldness immediately enveloping him. Kijo stood at the edge fixated on Hakana drifting off. She watched until his silhouette disappeared over the edge of the waterfall.

Hakana's body plummeted from the edge of the water fall crashing into the raging waters below. The unstoppable current mercilessly tossed him around with ease until his battered body washed up onto the distant embankment.

CHAPTER 6
SUNDERED BONDS

As the first light of dawn began to paint the horizon a soft orange, a cloaked figure trudged along the shallow riverbank. The figure's clothing was so dark it was difficult to discern their shape in the shadows of early morning. They carried a bucket in one hand and fishing rods in another.

The figure stopped in his tracks glancing over at the edge of the water. Hakana's body laid motionless in the early morning fog. The hooded figure quickly dropped his tackle and rushed over beside. Kneeling over Hakana, Iron Money's brow furrowed as he examines the injuries. He slowly focuses on each shallow breath and pale complexion, looking closely for any signs of life in the still body.

Iron Monkey was a seasoned warrior, with scars etched on his rugged face and calloused gorilla-like hands that had seen countless battles. He had a wild, ape-like appearance, with his dark charcoal fur and deep gray eyes. His two swords secured on his side.

Despite his fearsome appearance, Iron Monkey's heart was pure gold, and he possessed a deep well of compassion that extended to all those who sought refuge within their sanctuary. He had been through countless adversities, and each had only strengthened his resolve.

As he examined Hakana's lifeless body, his keen senses remained on high alert. Iron Monkey's instincts were finely honed, a result of years spent navigating the treacherous paths of war and survival. He scanned the area, searching for any signs of danger, for he knew that their camp was a fragile oasis in a world overrun by wickedness.

Iron Monkey scooped up the injured monk and began the arduous journey back to their camp, hidden behind the roaring waterfall, far from the prying eyes of Sifu's minions.

The camp, nestled amidst the lush greenery, had become a sanctuary for those who had escaped the clutches of tyranny.

Iron Monkey strides with purpose, his broad shoulders carrying a still form, drawing all the eyes of the camp to him. People on either side of him stopped and watched, standing still in silence as he slowly passed by them. He was a towering figure, with his two swords clanging against his back and charcoal fur rustling in the wind. His grizzled face is set in determination as he walks towards the medicine hut.

Standing up as she sees Iron Monkey pass by, Hana Kimura shadows Iron Monkey, her gaze alertly scanning the area for any sign of danger.

Hana Kimura, the immortal female samurai, possessed an ethereal beauty that transcended the boundaries of time. Hana's almond-shaped eyes, deep and mysterious, held the wisdom of ages, reflecting the indomitable spirit that resided within her.

Her hair, bright red, flowed around her face in soft waves and highlighted her exquisite features. Yet, beneath that delicate exterior, there was an unmistakable intensity in her gaze, a fire that spoke of countless battles and the resilience of a warrior who had faced the ebb and flow of centuries. In addition to her physical attributes, Hana Kimura's ability to tap into her deepest part of her chi allowed her to command powerful spells. She formed her hands into various mudras, gestures used in kundalini rituals, to create and manipulate powerful otherworldly energy.

Her attire was a seamless fusion of traditional samurai armor and a touch of supernatural elegance.

The armor, adorned with intricate designs, told stories of battles won and lost. The indigo hues of her robe whispered of moonlit nights and shadowy encounters, and the delicate embroidery depicted scenes from a bygone era, etched with the finesse of a master artisan.

Around her waist, a sash of crimson silk flowed like a river of blood, a stark contrast to the muted tones of her armor.

A katana, the blade glistening with a sheen, rested at her side—an extension of her very soul, its history intertwined with hers.

Hana Kimura follows to aid Iron Monkey into the medicine hut carefully lowering Hakana onto a raised cot. As he pulled away, the tattered robe fell from Hakana like a discarded shroud, revealing a bright crimson symbol scrawled across his chest. The skin around the design was burned and swollen.

Iron Monkey's eyes widen as they fixate on the ominous mark. He sucks his teeth and instinctively drew his sword as his suspicion was growing. He believed Hakana to be one of the demons they had long sought to vanquish. Reacting quickly, Hana Kimura, in her wisdom and compassion, stepped forward to challenge Iron Monkey's impending action.

"I do not sense malevolence emanating from this young man," she asserted gently, her voice filled with conviction. "His aura may be feeble at the moment, but I do not believe he poses a threat." She held her hand out, a plea for reason in her eyes, her determination to spare Hakana's life unwavering.

As Hana Kimura's eyes met Iron Monkey's, the silent plea echoed through the stillness. Her hand, suspended in the golden air, seemed to hold the delicate balance between life and death, a testament to the fragile threads that connected the destinies of those within the medicine hut. The sun, having completed its ascent, cast its benevolent gaze upon this pivotal moment, as if lending its cosmic weight to the silent plea for mercy.

In the early morning light, the air inside the medicine hut hung heavy with the aroma of healing herbs and the weight of impending decisions. The sun casting a warm, golden glow that filtered through the bamboo walls, creating patterns of light and shadow that danced on the tatami mats.

Iron Monkey, a formidable figure, loomed on the opposite side of the medicine hut, his countenance hidden beneath the shadows of a bamboo hat. The blade of his katana gleamed ominously, catching the warm sunlight that filtered through the walls. He knew that she was wise, and her intuition had never failed them, but his gut instinct told him otherwise.

Slowly, he began to lower his sword and nodded at Hana Kimura. "Very well. We will keep a close eye on him, but for now, we must tend to his wounds."

An unconscious Hakana lay still on the table, his exposed skin pale from blood loss. Wounds crisscrossed his body, a testament to the relentless fury of the demonic adversary.

The most threatening of his injuries lay on his stomach—a gaping slash that hinted at the possibility of fatal consequences. The edges of the wound were ragged, the skin around it bruised and discolored, revealing the profound impact of the demon's blade. Blood oozed from the laceration, staining Hakana's clothing and the floor beneath him, a grim reminder of the life force steadily seeping away.

As if the wounds from the demon's katana were not enough, Hakana's body also bore the marks of a treacherous fall over the waterfall. His bones, once sturdy and unyielding, now betrayed the toll of gravity's merciless pull. Some were broken, a symphony of fractures that echoed the severity of his descent.

Hana Kimura carefully laid out various herbs and roots on the table, her eyes narrowing to focus as she considered what was needed. Her fingers moved swiftly as she mashed and mixed them together in a bowl until they formed a thick, dark paste. Taking a damp cloth from the basin of water, Hana Kimura gently applied the paste to Hakana's wounds.

Iron Monkey reached for a handful of the herbal mixture, packing it tightly into Hakana's deep wounds before stepping back to allow Hana Kimura to take over. She pulled out a needle and thread, her hands steady as she skillfully sewed straight lines across each wound.

As Hana Kimura sewed the wounds shut, Iron Monkey took a cloth dipping into a fresh bowl of water. He hovered the damp rag over Hakana's severely chapped lips squeezing the cloth. Fresh water droplets fell upon Hakana's dry lips and mouth to help rehydrate the battered monk.

As Hana finished the last of her meticulous sewing, Iron Monkey stepped forward, his movements deliberate and controlled. With a touch that belied both strength and gentleness, he began the intricate task of realigning each broken bone within Hakana's battered body.

The room was motionless as Iron Monkey continued his work - his fingers pressing against the damaged flesh with familiarity. Low pops and clicks mix together, the sound of the necessary agony on the path to healing.

After tending to Hakana, the two placed him in a comfortable position to rest and heal. The hut was filled with the scent of sage incense and flickering candlelight. With Hakana now to rest, the two knew they had to inform their camp leader.

Iron Monkey, his bamboo hat casting a shadow over his features, moved with a quiet, measured confidence as he followed behind Hana Kimura to their leader's hut.

As they walked, the camp's inhabitants acknowledged their presence with humble bows and a chorus of muted reverence. Sunlight dappled through the leaves of nearby trees, creating shifting patterns of light and shade on the worn paths beneath their feet. The sounds of daily life in the camp—the clinking of metal, the distant murmur of conversations, and the occasional laughter of children—filled the air.

As they entered the hut, the ape-like figure was seated on a mat meditating. In the dimly lit interior of his secluded mountain hut, Sun Wukong, the Great Sage Equal to heaven, sat in deep silence. The small space was adorned with simple yet meaningful tokens of his life's journey, each carrying a story of trials and triumphs.

Sun Wukong's meditation posture was both regal and serene. His legs were crossed in the lotus position, and his muscular frame exuded an air of both strength and tranquility. His golden fur, as radiant as the sun at its zenith, contrasted beautifully with the earthy tones of the hut's wooden walls.

The Monkey King's eyes were closed, their depths concealing the boundless wisdom and the weight of the centuries he had witnessed. His strong, furrowed brow seemed etched with the memories of his adventures, his triumphs, and his tribulations.

In his right hand, he held his legendary staff, its name, Ruyi Jingu Bang, the ever-transforming staff that had served as both his weapon and a symbol of his mastery over cosmic forces. The staff, though shrunken in size during meditation, retained an aura of majestic power, its surface etched with intricate designs that spoke of its divine origins as it spun in place over his open right palm.

Around him, incense wisps curled gracefully, carrying with them the scent of ancient temples, and forgotten realms. The flickering candles on a nearby altar cast a warm, gentle glow, illuminating the sacred relics he had collected on his journey—a worn monk's robe, a weathered scroll of Buddhist scriptures, and a few treasured mementos from each of his masters.

As Sun Wukong sat in deep contemplation, his chest rose and fell in a steady rhythm, harmonizing with the ebb and flow of the natural world outside. The soft rustle of leaves and the distant hum of the rushing waterfall in the distance provided a soothing backdrop to his meditation, creating an aura of profound serenity.

Sensing Iron Monkey and Hana Kimura, Sun Wukong slowly opened his eyes, revealing a smug smile that danced at the corners of his lips. His gaze, which held the weight of centuries, met theirs with a playful glint.

"Well, well, if it isn't my dear friends Iron Monkey and the ever-curious Hana Kimura," he remarked with understated amusement, his voice carrying the resonance of ancient wisdom and the irreverence of a mischievous monkey. "I trust you've come seeking the wisdom of the Great Sage? Or perhaps just to bask in the radiant presence of one as magnificent as I?"

His tone was teasing, a reminder of the audacious spirit that had carried him through countless trials and encounters with the divine.

Hana Kimura teased back with playful sarcasm before saying, "we have found a wounded monk by the riverbank," Hana Kimura began, her voice low and respectful. "He bears a strange mark on his chest, and we are uncertain of his intentions."

Sun WuKong rose to his feet, towering over them with his imposing figure. He nodded; his golden eyes narrowed with a keen interest as he listened intently to their account.

"I see," he said thoughtfully, stroking his beard. "Bring him to me. Sun Wukong Requested.

Hana Kimura reported that the novice monk was unresponsive and in a precarious condition.

Hana Kimura and Iron Money both lead Sun Wukong to the wounded young man. As they entered the hut, the scent of herbs and incense filled their senses.

Sun Wukong's sharp eyes immediately fell upon the young man lying on the cot, his chest rising and falling in shallow breaths. Hana Kimura stood beside him, her expression one of concern and empathy. Sun Wukong circled the cot, his eyes scrutinizing the young man's injuries. He took in the sight of the deep wounds, the dark paste, and the steady stitches that held them together. He noted the wounds on his chest and the strange mark that glimmered in the candlelight.

Iron Monkey's eyes widened as he took a deep breath. He inhaled sharply and placed his hand on the hilt of his short sword. His muscles tensed with determination as he spoke firmly, "It is the mark of the Demon King. We must finish him."

Wukong stepped forward and placed a hand on Iron Monkey's shoulder. "Breathe, my friend," he said softly.

"It is not the mark of a demon, but that of a slave. The Demon King's sorcerers use dark magic and ancient totems to cast illusions over their victims that bear the marking they put on them making them vulnerable and easy to manipulate."

With confusion in his eyes. "Why not just enslave them with their might? Their power triumphs a human's easily." Iron Monkey pondered aloud.

Wukong smiled sadly and responded, "It is much easier to subdue someone when they don't even realize they're being controlled. A prisoner that believes they are free is less likely to resist Sadly, these slaves are just expendable pawns to the Ngok's Army."

Iron Monkey nodded in understanding, his grip on his sword loosening slightly. "What do we do now?" he asked, his voice laced with worry.

Wukong's eyes glinted with determination. "We need to find the source of this darkness and put an end to it," he said firmly. "But first, we need to heal this young man."

Hana Kimura stepped forward, holding out a bowl of herbal ointment. "This should help with his wound heal faster," she said softly, her gaze never leaving the young man's face.

Iron Monkey took the bowl from Hana and began to apply the ointment to the young man's wounds. As he worked, he couldn't help but feel a sense of sadness at the thought of all the innocent people being used as pawns in the endless war.

Wukong watched as Iron Monkey tended to the wounded youth, his mind already thinking of a plan to stop the Ngok Army from enslaving any more of the innocent people that were left within the region.

"Now we wait until he awakes." Sun Wukong states.

CHAPTER 7
ECHOES OF REDEMPTION

The sun and moon cycled several times before Hakana finally stirred from his deep slumber, eyelids fluttering open. He let out a long grueling moan as the pain of his wounds rushed back to him. Hana Kimura hurried to his side, her hand moving to soothe him with a gentle touch. "Take it easy," she said gently, touching his shoulder. "You must not overexert yourself or your wounds will reopen."

Hearing activity coming from within the medicine hut, Iron Monkey strides through the door, his movements full of purpose and determination. As Hakana lay still on the bed, Iron Monkey's gaze bore down upon him like a physical weight. Hakana's eyes widened in fear and his muscles tensed involuntarily at the sight of this imposing figure standing before him.

"Do not be afraid young monk. We mean you no harm." Iron Monkey spoke in a deep, commanding tone.

Hakana slowly sat up, wincing at the pain shooting through his body. He looked into Iron Monkey's eyes and saw a glint of kindness buried beneath the stern exterior. He nodded, indicating his understanding.

Hakana's spine stiffened as he took in the unfamiliar faces before him. He nervously cleared his throat and asked in a voice barely above a whisper, "Who are you?" His eyes darted around the room, never settling on any one person.

Hana Kimura and Iron Monkey stand side by side, their postures straight and proud, their expressions intense as they introduce themselves to Hakana. Their voices carrying an otherworldly resonance that Hakana had never seen before.

Hana Kimura speaks first, "We are the survivors of the Gnok's tyranny in this region. We escaped their oppression only to find ourselves here, in this camp, beyond the sacred falls."

Iron Monkey takes over, his gaze never leaving Hakana's face as he speaks. "We have been living here for months now and making do with whatever resources we can scrounge up. Our numbers are few, but our courage is strong."

Hakana looks around him in wonder, taking in his new surroundings as he waits for them to continue speaking. Through the doorway, he notices the makeshift tents scattered around.

Hana Kimura then turns her attention back to Hakana with an expectant look on her face. "Do you have the energy to walk?" she asked gently.

Hesitating for only a moment, Hakana replies "I think so." He slowly rises to his feet, feeling weak as he does so. Once standing, Hana Kimura and Iron Monkey take hold of Hakana's arms and guide him outside.

The sun beat down on Hakana's sore body, and though it hurt to breathe in deeply, the fresh air was a relief after so many days of confinement inside the hut. Before them lay a small encampment with around twenty occupants, all of whom had escaped from the oppressive forces emanating from the same temple Hakana had just fled.

The camp was bustling with activity as they walked through it--people cooking over open fires, children playing amongst themselves, elders gathered around talking animatedly about what had been left behind and where they should go next, their eyes momentarily distracted on the new face. They all looked upon the newcomer with curiosity. It was far too much for Hakana to take in all at once; he simply stood there staring wide-eyed at this place full of life and vibrancy that he hadn't truly seen since before the temple. And that was even somewhat of a blur for him at this time.

Iron Monkey turns to look at Hakana with an understanding smile on his face as if reading his mind, "We have all been through a lot, young monk. But we have found solace in each other's company and in the safety of this camp." Hakana looks up at Iron Monkey, touched by his words. "Thank you," he says softly.

Hana Kimura leads Hakana to a small tent at the edge of the camp. "You can rest here," she says, gesturing inside.

Hakana nods, grateful for the kindness of these strangers. As he enters the tent, he feels a wave of exhaustion wash over him. He collapses onto the bed and falls into a deep sleep, feeling safe for the first time in a long while.

Waking up hours later to hear the crackling of a fire and low mummers of conversation, Hakana slowly makes his way from his tent to see what was going on.

Iron Monkey and Hana Kimura gathered around the campfire, bathing in its warm, yellow light. Hakana, as if figuring out how to walk again, shuffles over to the burning fire and takes a seat next to Hana Kimura. She nimbly pulled the kettle from the fire and poured some fragrant tea into a wooden cup.

Offering it to Hakana with a bow of her head, she said "drink."

After a few moments of conversation amongst the three, Sun Wukong approached the fire with a imposing presence that froze Hakana in his tracks. Panic raced through Hakana's veins as he eyed the infamous creature, he heard stories about all his life.

"I've seen many monks in my time, but I've never before seen a shuffle monk". Sun Wukong chuckled at his own jest to lighten the mood and introduce himself to the unsuspecting newcomer at their camp.

Hakana let out a nervous laugh, relieved that Sun Wukong seemed to have a sense of humor. The young monk swallowed hard, unsure of what to say.

"I am Hakana," he said, still feeling wary of the creature before him.

He had always been taught to fear Sun Wukong as a tyrant, but now in his presence, all he could feel was curiosity and a strange sense of awe. Sun Wukong looked at Hakana with a glimmer of interest in his eyes. "Hakana," he repeated slowly, as if savoring the sound of the name. "You are from the temple, aren't you?"

Hakana nodded, feeling a lump form in his throat. He didn't know how much he should reveal to this creature who seemed to know more than he let on.

Sun Wukong stood tall, his deep laughter echoing off the trees surrounding them. His gaze was fixed on the young man before him, taking in every reaction. "Don't worry," he said in a comforting tone. "We all have our troubles, but here you will find people who accept and support you."

Hakana took a sip of the tea, letting the warmth spread through his body. He relaxed a bit, feeling more at ease in the presence of these people who had accepted him so easily.

As they sat by the fire, sharing stories and laughter, Hakana knew that he had found a new family in this unlikely group of strangers.

The time had come to unveil the grim history that had brought them together, the story of the Demon General Virote known to Hakana as Sifu and his malevolent spawns, and the cataclysmic events that had begun to plunge the Earth Realm into darkness.

Sun Wukong, the once-revered warrior, began the tale with a heavy heart. "Long ago, the Earth Realm was actually a place of harmony, where humans and immortals coexisted peacefully. The immortal protectors watched over our world, ensuring balance and safeguarding the innocent."

Iron Monkey's eyes bore the weight of years gone by as Sun Wukong continued, "But Virote, the demon general of unspeakable power, rose to prominence. With his spawns, he launched a sudden and devastating attack, slaughtering the immortal protectors and leaving our realm defenseless."

Hana Kimura listened intently, her eyes wide with a mixture of fascination and horror as she took in the story of the world's downfall. She had joined their ranks not long ago, drawn by the allure of their mission and the chance for redemption.

Monkey King's voice grew grimmer as he described their struggle to fight off the hordes. "Virote's attacks were relentless and cunning. He targeted our warriors without warning, leaving us no time to prepare for his onslaughts. Our people were forced into hiding, and our once-mighty order was reduced to remnants scattered across the Earth Realm."

Sun Wukong's face was etched with sorrow as he recounted their darkest days. "It was a time of despair, but it was also a time of resilience. Those of us who survived, like Iron Monkey and me, banded together in secret, hidden behind this very waterfall, training and preparing for the day when we could push back against Virote and the Ngok Army."

Hakana, the newest addition to their ranks, listened intently, absorbing every word. He had known pain and suffering, but the magnitude of the world's suffering under Virote's rule weighed heavily on him. It was a stark reminder of the importance of their mission.

As the fire crackled and the night deepened, Hakana realized that he had become part of something larger than himself, a brotherhood bound by a shared history and a collective purpose.

With the tale told and their spirits fortified, they knew that their mission was far from over. The legacy of Virote's tyranny still loomed large, and their path was fraught with challenges. But gathered around the campfire, they found strength in each other's company, knowing that they were united in their quest to bring light to a world shrouded in darkness.

Hakana, with newfound resolve, looked to his mentors with gratitude and determination. He had absorbed the lessons of their history, and he was ready to join them in the fight to reclaim their world and honor the memory of those who had fallen before them.

CHAPTER 8
IRON RESILIENCE

Reclined upon a plush bed of velvety furs, concealed within the sanctuary nestled behind the thundering cascade, Hakana found solace as Iron Monkey assumed the role of his mentor. His bamboo hat sat low just seated upon his brow, penetrating gaze of Iron Monkey delved deep into Hakana's very essence. The crisp mist emanating from the cascading waters enveloped them both, a comforting balm that gently assuaged Hakana's myriad aches and pains, creating an ethereal atmosphere in which he absorbed the sagacious counsel from his mentor.

Amidst the soothing embrace of the mist, Iron Monkey, resolute and unwavering, committed himself to more than just the physical healing of Hakana. His determination extended to the intricate task of reconstructing not only the monk's battered body but also the shattered strength of his spirit, fragmented by the unsettling revelations of his past.

The words imparted by Iron Monkey were not merely guidance but a profound effort to rebuild Hakana from the inside out, a testament to the mentor's commitment to fostering resilience and fortitude within his protege.

Iron Monkey would soon give the honor of passing on the wisdom of his sensei, the esteemed Miyamoto Musashi. He would be sure to include all the skill and mastery that had been gifted to him by his great master.

Miyamoto Musashi, known as a legendary ronin, philosopher and master of strategy, stumbled upon an unexpected encounter during one of his profound excursions. Deep within the dense forest, he discovered a toddler, crying with the pangs of hunger. In those crystalline moments, as their eyes met, Miyamoto perceived in the child a poignant mirror of his own history—a tale of loss, isolation, and the unrelenting challenges that carve one's fate. He was determined to guide and shape Iron Monkey into his supreme self.

Iron Monkey gingerly placed a hand on Hakana's trembling shoulder, acknowledging his fatigue and pain. The training began slowly, they started with simple exercises, stretching routines, yoga, and meditation to help Hakana regain his strength and focus. Each day was a small step towards recovery, a testament to Hakana's unwavering determination to reclaim his life.

The training area within the camp unfolded as a dynamic tableau of disciplined activity and focused determination. Surrounded by a lush thicket of towering bamboo, the air buzzed with the harmonious symphony of clashing wooden swords and the rhythmic footfalls of warriors engaged in rigorous exercises.

Shafts of sunlight filtered through the dense foliage, dappling the worn training ground with patches of golden warmth. The earth beneath bore the imprints of countless footsteps.

A gentle breeze stirred the leaves overhead, carrying with it the faint rustle of nature's chorus and the invigorating scent of the surrounding nearby trees. The training area seemed to exist in harmony with the natural elements, creating an atmosphere where the serenity of the bamboo forest merged seamlessly with the intensity of martial pursuits.

In one corner, wooden training dummies stood stoically, their surfaces scarred from the repeated strikes. Beyond them, a series of low wooden structures and obstacles hinted at the diverse training regimens—agility drills, balance exercises, and strength conditioning—that comprised the holistic approach to combat mastery.

Flags adorned with clan insignias fluttered in the breeze, adding splashes of color to the predominantly earth-toned surroundings. The vibrant symbols served as reminders of the diverse backgrounds and allegiances of the warriors who converged in this shared space to refine their skills.

The training area reverberated with the ringing of bamboo swords clashing together and the rhythmic thud of fists against wooden dummies with battered knuckles. Hakana's sweat-drenched brow glistened under the relentless sun as he followed the disciplines passed down by Miyamoto. Each day, he felt the burn in his muscles, the soreness in his limbs, but he persevered.

Iron Monkey understood that genuine advancement would necessitate pushing Hakana past his existing boundaries. As weeks unfolded from days, they initiated sparring sessions, transforming these practice bouts into a crucible for testing Hakana's resilience.

At the end of one afternoon training session with a gaze of fierce determination, Iron Monkey locked eyes with Hakana, conveying the initiation of their weapon training. He explained that their journey would commence with the traditional longsword—a weapon renowned for its lethal efficiency.

Without further warning, Iron Monkey hands Hakana a bamboo katana that feels light in his grip. But he knows better than to underestimate this blade and grabs it firmly with both hands as he's been trained to do in the past. The weight of the weapon feels reassuringly familiar as he holds it firmly and confidently in front of him.

Iron Monkey curled his lip in a smirk before lifting one leg with the strength of a raging gorilla. His right foot stood firmly planted on his left calf, providing stability.

"Knock me off balance." Iron Monkey insisted.

"Easy." Hakana stated in a low tone as he walked forward feeling cocky. Hakana sneered with predatory confidence as he stepped forward, both hands firmly gripping the bamboo katana. He unleashed a flurry of strikes against Iron Monkey in an attempt to end the fight quickly. But Iron Monkey effortlessly blocked each of his attacks and retaliated with a powerful attack that sent Hakana off balance as he tumbled to his side.

"Again!" Iron Monkey demanded!

Hakana's face burned with humiliation as he tried and failed to gain an edge on his opponent. He attacked wildly, desperation fueling his frenzied assault. But Iron Monkey was effortlessly in control, anticipating each of Hakana's moves like a chess master. Their swords clanged against each other over and over again, and still Iron Monkey stood firm.

Exhausted and disheartened, Hakana comes to a halt and questions what he may be doing wrong. "I've trained my whole life; I should be able to at least knock you off balance!"

Iron Monkey's foot hit the dirt with a heavy thud, "Your grip is wrong." He stepped closer to the monk, his full weight of his body behind the swing. with the blade in front of him. The wooden blade split the air in front of him. Hakana's hair fluttered as the air whipped past him from the swing and the gusts caressing his cheeks.

Iron Monkey goes on to explain the advantages of using one hand to grip the long blade. This gives you more maneuverability and steadies your stance, making it harder for your opponent to knock you off balance. It also allows you to fight with two weapons in certain circumstances.

Hakana released one of his grips readying his sword. Despite Hakana's best efforts, he found himself constantly outmaneuvered and overpowered. Iron Monkey was relentless, demonstrating the vast gap in their skills and experience.

Hakana's missteps cost him his opponent's end of the bamboo sword to catch him. Although wood, the bamboo sword still was excoriating to be stunned by. Hakana's frustration grew with each defeat, and doubt began to creep into his mind.

One evening, after yet another spar that ended with Hakana on the ground, gasping for breath, he lay there, defeated, and disheartened. Thoughts of giving up, of abandoning the path of a warrior, began to cloud his mind.

Iron Monkey, ever vigilant and perceptive, approached Hakana with a knowing look in his deep gray eyes. He extended a hand, offering it to his protege. "Hakana," he said softly, "I know it's tough, but remember, the path of a warrior is not forged in victory alone. It is also paved with defeat and the determination to rise again."

On his back, Hakana hesitated for a moment. The memories of his time in the temple flooded back. The agonizing memories seared into his consciousness like a burning iron, the screams of his friends echoing as they were ripped away from him. He was powerless to stop it, paralyzed with grief and torment. His friend's faces were imprinted in his mind, motivating him to keep going no matter the cost and never forget why he must continue forward on this path.

Hakana reached his arm out, hand hovering in the air. Then, with a firm resolve, he grasped Iron Monkey's hand and pulled himself up. The weight of his doubts still pressed upon him, but he was not ready to surrender.

Iron Monkey nodded in approval, recognizing the strength of character within Hakana. "You have the heart of a warrior. You've already faced the darkest truths of your past, and now, you must face the darkness within yourself. Only then can you truly emerge as a samurai, strong in body, mind, and spirit."

Their training continued, more intense than ever. Hakana's defeats did not diminish, but his determination to persevere grew stronger with each passing day. He learned from his losses, adapting, and evolving his techniques. Iron Monkey, in his unwavering support, began to provide more guidance and less resistance, allowing Hakana to bridge the gap between them slowly.

As the days turned into weeks, Hakana's strength, both physical and spiritual, began to shine through. The defeats that had once haunted his dreams were now sources of inspiration, reminders of the resilience that had brought him back from the brink of despair.

And so, under the watchful eye of Iron Monkey and the great teachings of Miyamoto Musashi, Hakana continued to train, driven by an unyielding determination to become the samurai warrior he had always aspired to be. Each spar, each setback, only steeled his resolve, and he knew that the path ahead would be challenging, but it was a path he was determined to walk until the end.

CHAPTER 9
SHATTERED CHAINS

Hakana's muscles, once rigid with inexperience, now rippled with the fluidity of a seasoned warrior. Iron Monkey's rigorous regimens had sculpted his body into an instrument of precision and power. Yet as he stood before Sun Wukong, an aura of anticipation enveloping him, it was clear that the terrain ahead was one of shadowed valleys within his own psyche.

"Your body is a fortress," Sun Wukong observed, his voice steady as the ancient hills, "but we must now explore the inner sanctum, where darker beasts lurk."

Hakana nodded, understanding that the greatest battles are often fought within the silent chambers of the soul. He could feel the unspoken fears, the

memories that clung to him like shackles,
threatening to drown him in their depths.

"Master Wukong, I am ready," Hakana affirmed,
though his heart raced at the thought of confronting
his past demons.

Sun Wukong's eyes narrowed, the gravity of their
task mirrored in his gaze. "The Gnok's tentacles
have been spreading unchecked," he stated
ominously. "We cannot afford the leisure of
traditional methods."

"Then how?" Hakana asked, his brow furrowing
with concern. He had always thought mastery of the
mind came from silent contemplation, not haste.

"Time is a luxury we do not possess," the sage
replied. "Hence, we shall use a different key to
unlock your potential." He gestured toward the
steaming pot that Hana Kimura had left for them.
"Mushroom tea," he said, "a catalyst for rapid
transformation."

Hakana's nostrils flared as he took in the pungent
aroma, feeling a slight tremor of trepidation. To
drink such a brew was to step into the unknown, to
relinquish control to the hands of fate and trust in
his mentor's ancient wisdom.

"Will it be safe?" Hakana's question hung in the air,
mingling with the steam from the tea.

"Safe?" Sun Wukong chuckled, the sound carrying both warmth and warning. "It will pry open the doors you've bolted shut deep within your subconscious, but fear not—within you lies the strength to face what emerges."

Taking the cup in his calloused hands, Hakana felt its warmth seep into his skin. His pulse thrummed in his ears, a drumbeat heralding a voyage into the recesses of his being. With a solemn nod to his master, he sipped the bitter liquid, bracing himself for the descent.

As the tea journeyed down his throat, a tingling sensation began to spread through his limbs, a whisper of the storm to come. Hakana closed his eyes, allowing the potion to saturate his consciousness.

"Let go, Hakana," Sun Wukong's voice was both a command and an incantation. "Release the chains of your history, and let the tea guide you to freedom."

With each heartbeat, Hakana's inner vista expanded, the walls of his mind stretching beyond the limits of his flesh. Colors swirled behind his eyelids, a kaleidoscope of his emotions painting the darkness. His breaths deepened, each inhalation a step deeper into the labyrinth of his memories.

"Master, I see... I see them," Hakana whispered, his voice a thread in the vast tapestry of his thoughts. He was there again, on that fateful night, the images sharp as broken glass. The pain, the loss—it gripped him with icy fingers, even as he sought the warmth of understanding.

"Face them, my pupil," Sun Wukong instructed, his tone a steady encouragement. "Face them, and in doing so, find your true self."

A shudder ran through Hakana's frame as he navigated the churning waters of his past. Sun Wukong's presence beside him was a bastion against the tide, a reminder that he was no longer alone.

"Rewiring" wasn't just a word—it was happening, synapses firing in new patterns, the front of his forehead tingling, old wounds beginning to stitch themselves anew. Hakana could feel it, a transformation not just of mind but of spirit.

"Let your inner eye open," Sun Wukong instructed, his voice now part of the landscape, a natural element that swayed with the trees.

Hakana felt the concoction deepening, spreading its influence through his veins. Sun Wukong and Hakana, two figures in meditative repose, were seated beneath the Bodhi tree, their legs crossed in the time-honored fashion of seekers of wisdom. The air was thick with the scent of the tea, an intoxicating blend that seemed to hold within it the whispers of the forest and the songs of the stars.

"Behold the canvas of your mind," Sun Wukong whispered, his voice a current in the visual symphony. The Monkey King stood resolute, a beacon amidst the chromatic storm, his eyes two moons of pure luminescence.

Together, they moved as one—two figures adrift in the dreamscape. With every step, the colors shifted, responding to the rhythm of Hakana's heartbeat. Memories flickered at the periphery of his vision: laughter shared, tears shed, moments both trivial and profound.

'These are my fears, my hopes,' Hakana thought, feeling the weight of years lifting from his soul. 'The echoes of who I once was.'

"Confront them," Sun Wukong instructed, pointing to a shadow that quivered in the distance. "Acknowledge them."

Hakana nodded, closing the space between himself and the darkness. As he approached, the shadow morphed, coalescing into a scene bathed in the golden glow of nostalgia. His chest tightened with emotion. It was a reflection of a time when innocence was his shield, before the world demanded the price of growing up.

"Every memory is a brushstroke in your portrait," the mentor intoned, his hand resting lightly on Hakana's shoulder. "What will yours reveal?"

"Strength," Hakana said, his voice firmer now, "and vulnerability."

"Good," Sun Wukong said, his silhouette shimmering with pride. "Embrace them both."

They continued onward, delving deeper. The landscape of Hakana's inner world twisted and turned, revealing hidden alcoves filled with whispers of the past. Each corner held a different shade of his psyche, a different fragment of his journey.

"Look beyond what you fear," Sun Wukong guided. "There lies your power."

'Can I truly be free of these chains?' Hakana questioned himself. Every step seemed to draw him closer to an answer, to a clarity that had eluded him for so long.

"Your thoughts are the architects of your reality," came the sagely reply. "Mold them as you wish."

Hakana watched as the vibrant energy around him began to pulse with a rhythmic certainty, aligning with his newfound resolve. Here, in the heart of his own universe, he discovered a tranquility that had always been just out of reach.

The ancient Bodhi tree stood tall in the moonlit clearing, its leaves whispering secrets of the ages as Hakana and Sun Wukong rested beneath its sprawling canopy. The air was thick with the scent of earth after rain, a testament to the night's revelations.

Sun Wukong's face, usually an enigmatic mask, softened into a smile, the creases around his eyes etched with pride. "You have embarked on a remarkable journey, my friend," he said, voice resonant with wisdom earned over lifetimes. His gaze held Hakana's, unwavering. "Remember what you have learned this evening and carry it with you always. Your mind is now a sanctuary of strength and resilience."

The words settled over Hakana like a mantle. He nodded, the motion releasing a cascade of emotions that pooled in his eyes, spilling over in silent tears of gratitude. "That was intense," he exclaimed, his voice trembling with the magnitude of his inner voyage. The young monk's hands, so often clenched in combat or poised in meditation, unfolded in his lap, palms open and receptive to the universe's vast energies.

He could still feel the tendrils of the mystic mind brew curling through his consciousness, a serpentine dance of enlightenment. Memories once shrouded in darkness now bathed in light, their sharp edges smoothed by understanding and acceptance. The revelation surged within him—a tide of power tempered by tranquility.

As Hakana wiped the moisture from his cheeks, a small, knowing grin played at the corners of his mouth. Internally, he marveled at the duality of his being—warrior and monk, strength, and serenity. He felt the gentle weight of Sun Wukong's hand on his shoulder, grounding him to the present moment.

"Your guidance is a gift I will never take for granted," Hakana murmured, turning his head slightly to acknowledge the touch. He sensed the shift in the air, the subtle change in energy as the world around them seemed to acknowledge the depth of his transformation.

"Let your actions reflect your newfound clarity," Sun Wukong advised, his hand lifting from Hakana's shoulder as he rose gracefully to his feet. The moonlight caught in his eyes, casting them aglow with celestial fire.

Hakana watched the silhouette of his mentor against the backdrop of the night sky, feeling the last of the brew's effects ebb away like the tide retreating from the shore. His heart pounded a steady rhythm, a drumbeat heralding his readiness to face whatever lay ahead.

"Master, how do I repay you for this?" Hakana asked, though he knew the answer before Sun Wukong spoke.

"Repayment comes in living out the lessons learned, in succeeding where once you might have failed," Sun Wukong replied.

Hakana found his feet, his legs steady as roots delving into the earth. They stood side by side, two figures cast from the same mold of determination and courage.

"Go on back to the campfire with the others," Sun Wukong suggested, nodding towards the distant glow, where their companions awaited their return.

Hakana agreed, his steps sure and purposeful. The shadows danced upon his path, flickering like the flames of destiny that burned within him. With each stride, he felt the echo of the past intertwining with the promise of the future, and he embraced it fully, ready to wield his mind's newfound sanctuary as deftly as he wielded his sword.

As he reached the campfire, it was just Hana Kimura sitting with her thoughts. Everyone else seemed to have drifted off to bed. Hakana joined Hana Kimura, the fire crackled and popped, tossing embers into the night like fleeting stars born from the earth.

Hakana settled beside Hana Kimura, feeling the embrace of the fire's warmth as it warded off the creeping coolness that clung to the edges of darkness. They sat in silence, two warriors bound not by words but by a shared heartbeat thrumming with anticipation for the challenges ahead.

Hakana watched the flames dance—a ballet of orange and yellow—and felt their light play across his features, painting him in the hues of resolve and purpose. The fire's glow cast a golden sheen on Hana's visage, highlighting the sculpted lines of determination that framed her face.

"Good session, Hakana?" Hana Kimura inquired, her voice a gentle melody that mingled with the nocturnal symphony of the forest.

Hakana mirrored her calm demeanor, a serene smile gracing his features. "Yes, indeed. Sun Wukong's teachings on the fortitude of the mind have been enlightening. Each lesson reveals layers of wisdom that I never thought possible."

Hana Kimura's eyes held a thoughtful gleam as she listened. The camaraderie of the campfire lent an intimate air to their conversation. "Sun Wukong is an ancient being, Hakana. His wisdom spans centuries. He has faced trials, conquered demons, and emerged wiser with each passing age."

Hakana's curiosity sparked. He gazed into the dancing flames, his eyes reflecting the flames' mesmerizing dance. "I wonder, how does one amass such wisdom? How has Sun Wukong become so wise?"

Hana Kimura sighed, her gaze distant for a moment as if recalling a tapestry of memories. "Wukong's wisdom is not just about time. It's about embracing experiences, learning from both victories and defeats. His journey has been one of self-discovery, understanding the intricacies of the mind, and finding harmony within the chaos."

"Each flicker tells a story," Hana Kimura murmured, leaning closer, her voice a soft accompaniment to the symphony of crackling wood. "Stories of battles fought, of victories and losses."

Hakana turned to her, the shadows retreating from his eyes as he met her gaze. "And what of the tales untold?" he asked, his voice barely above a whisper, yet heavy with the gravity of unspoken history.

Hana Kimura leaned in, her eyes filled with empathy, as she began to recount the untold story of Sun Wukong's past to Hakana.

"Even legends have their secrets," Hana Kimura replied, her empathy shining through the darkness like a glitter. She reached out, her hand briefly touching his arm in a gesture of solidarity. "Sun Wukong, our enigmatic mentor, carries a past filled with such secrets."

"Many believe Sun Wukong to be a god, and in many ways, he possesses godlike qualities." Hana's voice was gentle, a stark contrast to the harsh truths she spoke. "But his life has been marked by a tragic irony, Hakana."

He turned towards her, the firelight dancing upon her features, illuminating the earnestness in her eyes. The shadows made her look as if she wore a mask of sorrow, one that told tales of struggles unseen and voices unheard.

"Despite his powers and his noble heart, the gods never truly accepted him," she continued, her fingers idly tracing patterns in the dirt beside the campfire. "He was considered an outcast, a being caught between two worlds."

Hakana felt a pang of kinship in his chest. He, too, knew what it was like to belong nowhere, to be suspended in a limbo of identity. He could see the parallel lines of their lives converging in a point of empathy.

"An outcast?" He swallowed the tightness in his throat, his voice barely above a whisper. "With all his might and wisdom?"

"Exactly because of it," Hana murmured, nodding slowly. "Strength can intimidate, and wisdom can challenge the status quo."

Within Hakana, understanding blossomed like a lotus in murky waters, casting light upon the murky depths of Sun Wukong's enigmatic existence. A deity shunned by his own kind was a deity bound to the earth, to its mortals, and their shared plight.

"When the Gnok army took over our region, it was a time of great turmoil and darkness," Hana's words pulled him back to the present, to the gravity of their situation.

"Sun Wukong, who holds the strength of a god, felt the weight of guilt upon his shoulders." Her eyes seemed to reflect the inferno before them, ablaze with the intensity of the memory. "He believed he could have saved those around him, could have fought off the Demon General Virote, but he couldn't. In his eyes, he had failed, and he was never able to forgive himself for it."

The fire crackled, a symphony of tiny sparks leaping into the velvet night.

"For all these years," she began, her voice a whisper woven with strength and sorrow, "Sun Wukong has been waiting for a chance to strike back, to let good triumph over evil." The shadows danced across her face as she spoke.

Hakana, seated on the cool earth beside her, felt his chest tighten. The weight of Sun Wukong's silent battles settled on him like the dark blanket of night. He yearned to understand the inner workings of such a storied being, to grasp the magnitude of what lay ahead.

"He yearns to avenge his fallen comrades," Hana continued, her gaze locked on the embers as if they could unveil the path forward, "and, most of all, to prove himself to the gods who cast him aside."

Hakana's hands clenched into fists, nails digging into his palms. The pain was grounding, a reminder that this was no mere tale but the narrative of a companion's tormented soul. In his mind's eye, he saw Sun Wukong—proud, powerful, yet touched by a poignant solitude that echoed through the ages.

A sudden gust of wind stirred the leaves around them, and Hakana watched as Hana Kimura braced against the chill. Her warrior's poise never faltered, even as strands of hair whipped across her face like banners in the wind. It was in this raw moment, between tales of legend and the bitter touch of reality, that the line between myth and man blurred.

"Does he seek forgiveness from the gods or from himself?" Hakana asked, his voice cracking the silence with the delicacy of a breaking branch.

"Perhaps both," Hana replied, turning her gaze towards him. Her eyes were pools of resolve, depths in which one could drown or find salvation. "But acceptance is a harder battle to win. For some, it is a journey longer than any war waged with sword and shield."

The echo of her words lingered in Hakana's mind. They coursed through him, a river of understanding carving its way through the bedrock of his resolve. This mission had become more than a fight against a tangible enemy; it was a crusade for healing the unseen wounds of the spirit.

"His determination... it's like a guide," Hakana murmured, half to himself, half to the night that cradled them both. "It's what drives us, isn't it? The hope that we might right the wrongs, not just out here"—he gestured to the darkness beyond the fire—"but in here." He tapped a finger against his chest, feeling the steady drum of his heart beneath.

"Exactly," she nodded, the corners of her mouth lifting in a smile that did not quite reach her eyes. "We fight for the day when acceptance is not a prize to be won, but a truth universally granted."

As the embers of the fire dwindled, casting a soft glow over the quiet campsite, Hana Kimura and Hakana felt the subtle shift in the night. The air carried the essence of a story well-told, and the time for words drew to a close.

Hana, her eyes reflecting the fading flames, gently concluded their storytelling session. "The fire wanes, Hakana. It seems our tales have found their natural end for tonight."

Hakana nodded, his gaze lingering on the dying embers. "Indeed, Hana.

The crackling of the fire transformed into a quiet murmur, and a serene hush settled over the campsite. The forest seemed to respond to the lull in conversation, offering its own nocturnal symphony—a chorus of rustling leaves, distant calls of creatures, and the soft whisper of the wind.

As the campfire relinquished its final flicker, In the silence that followed, Hana Kimura and Hakana, united by the stories woven around the campfire, embraced the peace of the night—a moment suspended in time, a chapter concluded, and the promise of a new dawn awaiting on the horizon.

The next few days unfurled like the petals of a lotus at dawn, each one revealing deeper layers of Hakana's untapped potential. Beneath the Bodhi tree, which stood as a silent witness to his metamorphosis, he and Sun Wukong entered into a sacred dance of mind and spirit.

"Feel the energy coursing through you," Sun Wukong instructed, his voice a low hum that vibrated with the rhythms of the earth. "It is your ally, the whisper of life that animates the universe."

Hakana closed his eyes, focusing on the pulse of power that thrummed in his veins. He could sense it now more than ever, a current that ebbed and flowed with his breathing.

"Good," Sun Wukong murmured, watching as Hakana's fists clenched and unclenched in rhythm with unseen tides. "Now, let go of the barriers. They are but illusions of your fears."

"Barriers..." Hakana echoed internally, visualizing the walls he had built around his heart, stone by stone. Each represented a memory of loss, a moment of pain, a sliver of regret. He took a deep breath, exhaling slowly, willing those walls to crumble.

"Imagine them falling away," the Monkey King prompted.

With a sharp exhalation, Hakana's mind pushed against the ramparts of his resistance. He imagined each barrier as a shadow before the rising sun, dissipating in the light of his willpower. Sweat formed on his brow, a testament to the inner battle waging within.

"Remember why we fight," Sun Wukong said, his voice cutting through the haze of effort. "For those who can no longer stand beside us. For a world that may one day understand the true meaning of acceptance."

"Acceptance," Hakana whispered, the word a mantra that fueled his resolve. The barriers shivered, cracked, and finally shattered into dust.

"Excellent," Sun Wukong praised, a smile gracing his stoic features. "You're learning to harness the strength of your convictions. It's a formidable force."

Hakana opened his eyes, feeling lighter, as if he had shed an invisible cloak of burdens. He looked at his hands, these instruments of both creation and destruction, and saw them anew. They were not just tools of combat; they were extensions of his very soul.

"Your journey has only just begun," Sun Wukong continued, his gaze penetrating. "The path ahead is fraught with perils, but also ripe with opportunity. You must rise to meet it, Hakana."

"I understand," Hakana replied, nodding with a solemnity borne of their shared experiences. Sun Wukong's past struggles, mirrored in Hakana's own, bound them together in purpose.

"Understanding is but the seed," Sun Wukong countered, his eyes locking onto Hakana's. "Now you must nurture it. Let it grow into wisdom that overshadows ignorance."

Hakana felt a surge of gratitude for his mentor's guidance, a wellspring of knowledge that seemed as infinite as the stars above. With each passing day under Sun Wukong's tutelage, he peeled back the layers of his own limitations, exposing the core of his being. The journey of the mind was strenuous, but with each barrier broken, he stepped closer to the warrior he was meant to become.

"Tomorrow, we shall test your progress," Sun Wukong announced, standing with fluid grace.

"Then when tomorrow comes, I'll be ready," Hakana declared, determination setting his jaw and igniting a fire in his chest. He would face whatever trials awaited with the ferocity of a storm and the calm of the deepest sea.

As the day's last light bled from the sky, painting it with strokes of indigo and gold, Hakana embraced the stillness of the evening. His thoughts turned inward, reflecting on the lessons learned and the barriers overcome. In the quietude, he found strength—a reservoir of untapped power waiting to be unleashed.

CHAPTER 10
VEINS OF DARKNESS

Sun Wukong, Iron Monkey, Hakana, and Hana Kimura set off from the safety of their camp and journeyed through the desert, high mountains, and now trudged through the floating forest. The ground beneath their feet was thick with decaying leaves that squelched and crackled under their weight. The air was heavy with the scent of damp soil, decaying vegetation, and something foul that reminded them of rotten eggs. The sky above was a deep shade of indigo, blocked out by the imposing darkness of the trees. It seemed to close in on them like an oppressive cloak, making it hard to tell if it was night or day. As they walked, they could hear strange sounds echoing through the woods—animal cries twisted into something unnatural, branches snapping under a weight beyond that of any beast, and whispers on the wind that sent chills down their spines.

Sun Wukong led the way, his agility allowing him to leap over fallen logs and duck under low-hanging branches with ease. His golden staff swung expertly at the vines that tried to wrap around his ankles or yank him back. Iron Monkey followed closely behind, his bare feet gripping the rough bark of the trees as he climbed nimbly from one to the next.

Hakana stayed near the back, his eyes peeled for any sign of danger. Hana Kimura brought up the rear, her bow at the ready, arrows nocked and drawn. Her keen senses warned her of approaching threats before they could strike.

The forest seemed alive itself, as if it was conspiring against them. The air was thick with humidity and sweat trickled down their backs despite the coolness of the evening. The ground squelched underfoot as they walked, the earth slick with a slippery substance that gave them the impression of walking on slime. The smell of decay filled their nostrils, making them wrinkle their noses in disgust. It clung to their clothes and skin, refusing to be washed away. As they pushed deeper into the forest, the vegetation thinned out, revealing a clearing ahead.

Finally, they emerged into the open air. A chill wind greeted them as they looked up at the sky filled with dark clouds moving fast. Thunder rumbled in the distance, and rain began to pelt them. They trudged forward through the pelting rain continuing their mission.

The path led them to a uniquely carved stone that held the divine weapon, a sword of immense power hidden inside a towering rock. The black blade gleamed with a celestial energy that made their skin crawl. As they approached it, they heard a rustling in the surrounding forest. Their worst fears were confirmed when a horde of demons sprinted from the shadows, heading straight for the weapon.

Their hearts pounded in their chests as they raced to reach the sword before the demons could get to it. But it was too late. The creatures were upon them, more numerous than ever before.

Suddenly, a palpable dread swept over them as the earth beneath their feet began to quiver and shake. All present were paralyzed, unable to comprehend the unfolding terror. The colossal roots and sinister vines, once tangled in chaos, began to weave together, rocks and trees warping and melding into a monstrous form, ascending skyward. The sound of immense trees snapping echoed through the forest as a terrifying creature took shape.

It was a dragon, born of the earth itself. Its scales were the color of dirt, its eyes two burning coals in its head, and its wings stretched out as far as the horizon. The towering beast lowered its gaze upon the encroaching Gnok Army. The stench of brimstone filled the air as the demons halted in their tracks, realizing what they were up against. The loathsome guardian, a dragon, poised itself to unleash unspeakable horrors upon those who dared to threaten the celestial weapon's sanctity.

The battlefield erupted into chaos, but this time the demons seemed different – more organized, more strategic. They swarmed around the group, appearing from every crevice and corner of the forest. Their shrieks and growls filled the air as they launched attacks from all sides.

In response, the dragon unleashed a torrent of fire upon the oncoming horde, incinerating scores of them in an instant. Still, they kept coming, driven by some wicked force. The stench of burning flesh mingled with the pungent smell of demonic magic in the air.

As the group fought desperately against the overwhelming odds, they felt the sword's energy coursing through them. It fueled their strength, allowing them to deflect blows and strike back with newfound ferocity. The metallic taste of blood filled their mouths, along with the tang of magic and demonic might.

The ground beneath their feet became a slick morass of blood and ash as the battle wore on. Bodies littered the forest floor. Yet still, the relentless assault continued. The dragon flamed and writhed, breathing fire and death upon the encroaching hordes as it fought to protect the relic.

The sky darkened as night fell deeper, casting eerie shadows over the carnage below. The moon hung low, its light reflecting off the dragon's scales in an angelic glow. Lightning flashed in the distance, illuminating the hellish scene for brief moments before plunging everything back into darkness.

The battle raged on for hours, turning the once-untouched forest into a charred wasteland. Yet still, the demons pressed forward. The group could feel the dragon tiring, its strength waning under the relentless assault. Its cries of pain and rage echoed through the night, a haunting anthem of resistance against the forces of darkness.

On the battlefield, the earth dragon continued its rampage against the remaining demons. With every step, its massive tail crushed those who dared get too close, while its wings sent waves of panic through the rest. The ground trembled under its weight as it stalked through the ravaged landscape, its eyes glowing illuminating with an unholy rage.

The air was filled with the sickening squelch of bodies being crushed beneath its powerful form as it moved, seeking out the last of its enemies.

Iron Monkey weaved in and out of the clashing armies, his movements swift and sure. He leapt through the air, dodging blades and spears as he spun his swords around himself, deflecting attacks. He was a blur of motion, his acrobatics mesmerizing as he shot towards the dragon's side, cleaving through its scales with precision strikes. Its head whipped back and forth in search of its attacker, but Iron Monkey was already gone, moving too quickly for even its eyes to follow.

Hana Kimura stepped forward; her arms raised high. Her voice resonated with ancient incantations, calling forth otherworldly chains of light that weaved around the dragon' s limbs, binding them tightly. She could feel the dragon's power, its unyielding strength, but she held fast, determined to keep it from harming her fellow warriors. The chains glowed with an ethereal radiance that illuminated the battlefield, casting eerie shadows on the bloody ground.

With each passing moment, the dragon struggled against her bindings, it's terrible roars shaking the very earth beneath their feet. Its scales were as tough as iron and its muscles as strong as steel, yet she held on. She could feel the strain, but she would not let it break free, not while they were still within striking distance.

In response, Sun Wukong launched himself at the beast, his energy crackling around him like lightning, his staff glowing bright as he struck at the dragon's underbelly. With a mighty blow, he sent fragments of scale armor scattering in all directions. The dragon roared, its breath searing hot as it tried to breathe fire upon him, but he was already gone, dancing away with impossible agility.

They worked in tandem, each strike drawing the dragon's attention farther from the horde. They could feel its rage growing, its fury intense, but they remained undeterred. They had a common goal, and they would achieve it together.

Sweat trickled down Iron Monkey's face, exhaustion setting in as he continued his relentless assault. He leapt higher, spinning through the air, landing several strikes before disappearing again. His heartbeat like a drum, his breathing labored.

The dragon turned its head targeting its next victim and, in that moment, Sun Wukong knew their time was up. With one final burst of speed, he leapt higher than ever before, using his spinning staff lifting him high into the sky, landing right on its horn, and plunging his staff deep into the beast's glowing eye. It shrieked, thrashing violently as it descended back to the ground. The vines began slowly slithering back into their place, the stone scales crumbled down as the fire of its eyes diminished.

Hana Kimura lowered her arms, falling to her knees out of pure exhaustion. The chains of light dissolved, leaving only a faint hum in the air to mark their passing.

As dawn broke, the last of the demon horde disappeared into the shadows, leaving behind a scene of utter devastation. The group stood, battered, and bruised but victorious. Sun Wukong approached the rumble. The earth still moving slowly back into place, leaving within the rubble, the divine blade. The Monkey King leaned over grabbing the ancient weapon from within the rubble. The blade made of onyx-like in material. Its blade serrated and unlike traditional blades.

Sun Wukong walked over to Hakana handing him the powerful weapon. "This is yours, Hakana," Sun Wukong said, his voice a low rasp of exhaustion. "Guard it well."

Hakana took the sword with a wide-eyed reverence, the weight of it far heavier than he anticipated. He traced the serrated edge with his fingers, marveling at the cool touch of onyx. It was ancient yet there was an inexplicable feeling of vitality emanating from it.

As the sun began to rise, the group finally took stock of their surroundings. The battlefield was a desolate wasteland, charred and barren where lush foliage and towering trees once stood. The ground was littered with smoldering bodies of fallen demons and splintered remnants of what once were proud trees.

Despite the devastation around them, they couldn't deny the sense of triumph that surged within them. They had faced an army of demons, fought an earth dragon, and lived to tell the tale. They had protected the celestial weapon from falling into wrong hands and possibly saving their world.

But they also knew their work was far from over. There would be more battles to fight in the days to come, more enemies to conquer.

They exchanged a few more words before heading back through the floating forest. Hakana carried the weapon in a tight grip, its mystifying glow lighting up his face. Exhausted from their adventure but filled with satisfaction and strength, they trudged through the rugged terrain for miles, the promise of camp nagging at them like an itch no one could scratch. But even as dangers lurked in the shadowy corners of the forest, their hearts were lightened by a shared sense of heroic pride.

CHAPTER 11
NIGHTMARE'S EMBRACE

The journey back to the camp with the ancient
weapon was truly awe-inspiring. The setting sun
painted the sky in shades of gold, orange, and fiery
red, making the warriors look like divine beings as
they marched through the winding paths of the
forest. The thudding of their feet against the ground
resonated with each step they took, followed by the
clinking of metal and the occasional rustling of
leaves.

The air was thick with anticipation; it felt like time
itself stood still for this momentous occasion. As
they approached the clearing, the scent of smoke
and roasting meat filled their nostrils, mingling with
the earthy scent of the forest. The quadlet, its sleek
frame glistening under the fading light, hummed in
harmony with the excited chatter around it.

Suddenly, a cheer erupted from the camp, loud and reverberating, echoing off the trees and sending birds flying into the sky. The drums started beating furiously, and the flames in the bonfire burst higher, illuminating faces aglow with wonder and excitement.

The warriors halted before the camp entrance, weapons held high, and revealing the precious cargo they had brought - the ancient weapon, a relic thought to be long lost.

Amidst the chaos, an elderly figure emerged from a tent, his ink-stained hands held up in a sign of peace. His eyes widened at the sight of the weapon, and he approached slowly, gingerly reaching out to touch its surface as if afraid it might crumble under his touch. He murmured prayers under his breath, his wrinkled face contorted into a mix of awe and reverence. The crowd parted to let him pass, respecting his age and wisdom.

A cook, her face smeared with soot and sweat from tending to the fire, turned a spit of roasting meat, releasing a wave of enticing aromas that made stomachs rumble in unison. The meat sizzled and popped, tempting them all to abandon their posts for a taste. Yet, for now, they remained transfixed by the gift before them.

Sun Wukong who had led the expedition, his heart heavy but proud, addressed the crowd. "We bring you the divine weapon!" their voice boomed above the clamor, "a symbol of our bravery and courage. It is our hope that it will protect us from harm and guide us towards victory."

Another cheer went up, this one louder than before, and people started dancing around the bonfire, clapping, and stomping their feet. Children ran around, laughing and shrieking in delight, while the elders conferred amongst themselves in hushed tones. Music filled the air, drums beating faster, flutes playing melodies that stirred something primal within them all.

Under the canopy of stars, the drums began to beat out a rhythm that resonated within their very souls. It was a primal call to action, a reminder that they were stronger together. As they danced and sang under the stars, their voices rising in unison, the sound vibrated through the night sky, echoing off the surrounding cliffs. It was as if the universe itself was cheering for them.

They feasted on roasted venison and wild fruits, drank honeyed mead from hollowed-out gourds. Giggles and laughter rang out as children, their small hands sticky with berry juice, chased each other through the camp. Their innocence was a welcome distraction from the grim reality they had left behind. Overhearing the teasing banter between young siblings, Hakana couldn't help but smile.

As the night wore on, weariness settled in, and one by one, warriors retreated to their huts to recharge.

Hakana found himself growing drowsy as well. He curled up next to the fire, gazing at the dance of flames. A soft rustling at the edge of his awareness broke through the haze. Opening his eyes, he saw a small figure approaching. A child, no more than eight summers old, carefully carrying a braided bracelet made from twigs and grass. Tentatively, she extended it towards him. "For you," she whispered, her eyes shining with reverence.

Hakana's heart swelled with emotion as he reached out to take it, feeling the rough cord against his fingertips. "Thank you," he said. The child runs back to her mother following her back to their hut.

Bringing his attention back to the dancing flames, a veil of melancholy fell over Hakana as he missed his friends, the shared laughter, and the valiant spirit that had once defined their collective journey. Jade, with her fierce determination; Quon, the steadfast pillar of support and an older brother figure; Kaleb, whose humor had been a flicker of light in the darkest moments—each face etched in his memory.

He couldn't help but wish they were there to partake in the festivities, to revel in the triumph that now illuminated the camp. The void left by their absence lingered, casting a shadow over the celebration, and Hakana couldn't escape the feeling of emptiness that accompanied his recollections. He longed for the familiar presence of his departed friends.

For a brief moment, Iron Monkey diverts his attention and rests his hand on Hakana's shoulder. He smiles and nods, communicating without words. Hakana understands the unspoken message from Iron Monkey. With a heavy heart, Hakana brings his attention back to the celebration, letting the laughter and music envelop him. In the flickering shadows of the bonfire, he carried the memories of his lost friends, feeling their presence in the echoes of celebration and determination that resonated throughout the camp.

Suddenly, a dark presence disturbed his tranquility; a familiar devilish laugh rang out, sending chills down his spine. "Kijo..." he whispered under his breath. Before anyone could react, she materialized before them. Children ran in terror as the music stopped abruptly, replaced by the collective gasp of the crowd. Her tattered kimono floating slightly as she hovered, her long black hair dancing in the faint light from the bonfire. Fiendish creatures poured forth, their arrival marked by deep chuckles and otherworldly growls, as she chanted an unholy, ancient incantation.

"Protect the camp!" Hakana roared, drawing his sword as portals opened up around Kijo, spitting forth more of her twisted minions.

The once-celebratory camp, now caught in the grip of terror, faced an impending onslaught, and the air itself seemed to thicken with the impending doom.

The jubilant atmosphere shattered like fragile glass as panic seized the camp, the revelry replaced by a frenzied scramble for safety. Unprepared and unequipped, Hakana and the immortals, caught in the disarray, sought desperately for their weapons— a futile attempt to arm themselves against their immediate threat.

As the panic escalated, the air grew thick with the stench of fear, a putrid odor that clung to the skin like a malign residue. Shadows morphed into grotesque shapes that seemed to writhe with a sinister life of their own.

The nightmarish onslaught unfolded with a ghastly ferocity as the vile creatures, born from the darkest depths of hell, tore into their victims with an insatiable hunger for suffering. Screams, raw and primal, sliced through the night, reaching a crescendo of agony that seemed to echo into the abyss. Each cry carried the weight of desperation, a futile plea for reprieve from the unrelenting onslaught.

The air crackled with an unholy energy as Kijo made her way through the chaos, her movements seemingly synchronized with the relentless carnage around her. The creatures, extensions of her malevolence, carved through the camp's defenders with an otherworldly precision, leaving a trail of carnage in their wake.

She reached for the divine weapon, her grip unyielding, and in a surge of inky darkness, she was swallowed by the black night, taking with her the only hope that had graced the forsaken place.

With heavy hearts and tormented souls, the quartet fought valiantly, carving through the malevolent creatures that sought to state their ravenous hunger for suffering.

Hakana, who had tasted the bitterness of captivity and loss, was particularly devastated, his eyes shimmering with unshed tears as he surveyed the desolation. In this heartbreaking moment, the immortals and Hakana shared a profound sense of anger and sorrow, as they vowed to avenge the village and to reclaim the stolen relic.

The final battle awaited them at the dark temple, a nightmarish confrontation with Kijo and the malevolent forces that had shrouded their world in darkness for too long. With a heavy resolve, they rested, preparing their scarred bodies and their shattered spirits for the agonizing trial that lay ahead.

CHAPTER 12
VEIL OF THE RISING SUN

Fueled by a determination that blazed like an unquenchable inferno, Sun Wukong, Iron Monkey, Hakana, and Hana Kimura forged a meticulous plan to infiltrate the ominous temple. Their collective goal: to reclaim the sacred relic weapon and extinguish the nightmarish reign of General Virote and Kijo's malevolent wrath.

Each step led them through a terrain where sinister forces festered, and the very air seemed to crackle with an intangible malice. It was a calculated gamble, a perilous dance with the shadows, as they prepared to confront the darkness that lurked within the temple's foreboding walls.

As they approached the entrance, Sun Wukong stopped and held up his hand. He closed his eyes and took a deep breath, trying to sense any traps or hidden dangers within. The wind picked up suddenly, carrying with it the scent of decay and the distant howl of wolves in the distance.

A warm breeze carried the scent of sulfer and rot towards them. A putrid smell that made everyone's eyes water slightly. Whispers started; they were loud, more insistent. Demons were coming - many demons. And they were closing in fast.

The walls groaned and creaked as if something terrible was about to emerge from its bowels. Sun Wukong swore under his breath, "They know we're here," he muttered through gritted teeth.

"We fight or we die here." Hakana replied, his eyes darting between the shadows, searching for any sign of movement.

With a unified front, they charged into the darkness. Under the shroud of night, their every step was marked by the weight of their mission. The stakes were incomprehensibly high, for the celestial weapon was their solitary glimmer of hope in the eternal blackness that had besieged their realm.

The four were like wraiths, slipping through the shadows and striking with precision and deadly speed. Demon's bodies dropped to the ground in mere seconds, their crimson blood painting the walls behind them in sickly fashion. They moved with an urgency to even the playing field, each one ready for the inferno that was sure to follow.

Iron Monkey and Hakana, forces of nature, plunged headlong into the heart of the grotesque horde of demons, their every movement a symphony of destruction. The air sizzled with an aura of impending violence as their sharp blades became an extension of their unyielding will.

The demons, their twisted and grotesque forms clashing with the unstoppable warriors, were no match for their unparalleled skill and agility. With every strike, their weapons, a blur of motion, bludgeoning, impaling, and cleaving through their wretched ranks. It was a deadly ballet, a dance of chaos and death where each step brought another gruesome execution.

Iron Monkey, with his long and short blade out, whirled through the air, a tempest of destruction that sent demons sprawling, limbs severed, and bodies shattered. He leaped and somersaulted, moving with a fluidity that defied the laws of physics, never hesitating in his brutal onslaught.

The demons, clawed and gnashed at Hakana, but his instincts and reflexes were honed to perfection. His every parry and counterattack was a lesson in the art of combat, leaving a trail of dismembered and disfigured foes in his wake.

As the battle raged on, Iron Monkey's and Hakana's struggles were a testament to the relentless onslaught. Blood spattered their attire, and their breath came in ragged gasps, but they refused to yield. With each swing of their swords, the demons paid a gruesome toll, their agonized screams echoing through the accursed battlefield.

Iron Monkey's gruesome executions continued without mercy, a whirlwind of destruction and retribution. Limbs and heads rolled, torsos were impaled, and the ground became slick with the lifeblood of the fallen. It was a sight of unrelenting horror and butchery, a testament to the indomitable spirit of the Iron Monkey.

The grotesque hordes could not withstand the storm of fury and skill that came from Hakana, and in the end, it was they who met their gruesome demise at his hands.

As Hana Kimura stood, her eyes blazing with righteous fury, she could feel the air around her grow cold and oppressive. Shadows swirled and twisted, coalescing into a sinister form that gradually took shape before her. The shadows seemed to twist and contort, and the air grew heavy with a palpable sense of dread.

Amidst the gathering darkness, a figure emerged, clad in a sinister, flowing gi that seemed to absorb the very light around it. Kijo, the embodiment of spite, floated just above the ground, her feet never touching the earth. Her eyes were twin orbs of maleficent energy, glowing with an unholy radiance that pierced through the darkness.

Kijo's presence was heralded by an eerie, discordant chorus of whispers and invocations that seemed to emanate from the very fabric of reality itself. These ghostly voices spoke in an ancient, arcane language, their words a cacophony of darkness that sent shivers down the spines of all who heard them.

The battle that followed was a horrifying spectacle, a clash of elemental forces and dark sorcery. Hana Kimura's enchantments, an embodiment of her unyielding resolve and inner strength, collided with Kijo's dark sorcery, a malign force that sought to corrupt and consume all in its path.

With every incantation and gesture, the air crackled with supernatural energy. Bolts of dark lightning lanced through the battlefield, and tendrils of shadow slithered across the ground, reaching for Hana Kimura like serpentine tendrils of nastiness.

The two combatants weaved and danced through this nightmarish confrontation, each spell and counter-spell a crescendo in their relentless contest for mastery over the supernatural forces that bound them. The very earth seemed to groan and squirm beneath their clash, as if the world itself recoiled from the intensity of their battle.

Their battle was a collision of light and shadow, of good and evil, and it played out on a supernatural stage where the very fabric of reality trembled in the face of their power. As their conflict raged on, the fate of their world hung in the balance, and the echoes of their struggle reverberated through the dark temple, a testament to the relentless clash of opposing forces.

Hana Kimura, her voice resonated with power as she chanted ancient incantations, weaving her magic with graceful gestures. Beams of radiant energy lanced from her fingertips, streaking toward Kijo, who countered with a sinister, shadowy shield.

The magical duel continued with both combatants launching spells and counters in rapid succession. Waves of light and darkness collided, creating explosions of radiant energy shadows that illuminated the battlefield in an eerie dance of power.

As the fight intensified, both Hana Kimura and Kijo recognized the need to get up close and personal. Their incantations culminated in the unsheathing of swords.

Kijo, with her wickedness imbued in every movement, pressed the attack aggressively. Her dark blade sliced through the air with deadly precision, and Hana Kimura was forced into a defensive stance, parrying and dodging the relentless strikes taking damage as she tried deflecting her attacker.

Blood dripped from Hana Kimura's wounds down to her palms from the gashes left upon her skin. Seeing the blood from her soon to be victim, Kijo struck at her prey again viciously. Hana Kimura raised her katana, a dull thud echoed through the crowd as their swords met once more. Hana Kimura then took a step closer, angling for an opening. She felt it as soon as Kijo's breath hitched - an unguarded moment. Summoning the last of her strength with a lightning-quick maneuver, she thrust her blade upward, piercing through the bottom of Kijo's chin. The end of Hana Kimora's blade sticking from the top of Kijo's head. Blood tickled down her defeated foe's forehead before Hana Kimora slid her katana loose.

Kijo's body fell forward, her face slamming into the ground below. Hana Kimora stood over her, panting heavily, feeling the adrenaline surge through her veins.

The battlefield trembled as the clash between Sun Wukong, the Monkey King, and Virote, the formidable demon general, unfolded. The air snapped with an otherworldly energy, and the very ground seemed to groan in anticipation of the impending battle.

Sun Wukong, a legendary figure with his golden staff, stood with a confident smirk. Virote, the demonic general, loomed on the opposing side, clad in dark, ethereal armor and wielding the divine.

The two combatants locked eyes, and the tension hung thick in the air before erupting into violence. Virote lunged forward, his weapon gleaming with an ominous aura. Sun Wukong, ever agile and quick-witted, somersaulted into the air, avoiding the initial strike. He landed gracefully and swung his staff with incredible speed, aiming to exploit any opening in Virote's defenses.

Virote parried with his ancient weapon. The clash of their weapons echoed across the battlefield, and each strike sent shockwaves that cracked the very ground beneath them. The sky above seemed to darken as the battle intensified, a reflection of the cosmic struggle between light and darkness.

Sun Wukong, known for his supernatural abilities, summoned clones of himself, creating a chaotic dance of monkey warriors that confounded Virote.

However, the demon general, with his experience and unholy strength, cut through the illusions with relentless determination. The ancient weapon, now fueled by demonic power, cleaved through the air with deadly precision cutting down each clone brutally.

 The demon general, undeterred, unleashed dark magic, causing shadows to writhe and twist into monstrous forms that lunged at the Monkey King.

As the battle raged on, Sun Wukong's eyes glinted with determination. He unleashed his most powerful transformations, growing in size and strength.

Flames of divine energy surrounded him, enhancing his strikes and adding an otherworldly intensity to his attacks. Virote, undeterred, absorbed the dark energies around him, becoming a swirling tempest of demonic might.

The clash reached its peak, with each strike threatening to reshape the very fabric of reality. The world quaked around them, and the air shimmered with the residue of divine and demonic power colliding.

In a swift and calculated motion, Sun Wukong surged forward, his staff cutting through the air like a streak of golden lightning. The Monkey King's eyes gleamed with determination as he targeted the demonic grip holding the ancient weapon. The Ruyi Jingu Bang connected with a resounding impact, and the ancient weapon was sent hurtling out of Virote's grasp, spinning through the air before clattering to the ground.

At that precise moment, Hakana, swift and silent, slid towards the fallen weapon, his hand reaching out in synchronization with Virote's desperate attempt to reclaim it. The air crackled with tension as both combatants reached for the blade, fingers inches away from their goal.

 Hakana's fingers closed around the hilt of the ancient weapon just milliseconds before Virote's clawed hand could reclaim it. The Demon General, now disarmed, turned to face Hakana with fury.

Hakana's eyes flashed with an intensity fueled by the realization of his enslaved existence. The curse that had bound him to the Gnok Army was shattered, and a surge of newfound strength empowered his resolve raised the divine weapon high. The blade shimmered ominously, and with a single, swift slice, Hakana's strike carved through Virote's neck. A grotesque silence followed, broken only by the ghastly sound of flesh parting.

Virote, the once-terrifying reigning Demon General, stumbled backward. His once imposing form twisted and contorted, morphing into nightmarish figures that thrashed in agony. Shadows danced across the Demon General's morphing silhouette, and a guttural scream echoed through the desolate battlefield.

The horror was palpable as Virote's demonic essence unraveled, revealing the grotesque transformation that Hakana's strike had initiated. Nightmarish shapes clawed their way out from within, as if the darkness itself sought to escape the doomed vessel.

The once-demonic general, now a grotesque amalgamation of horrors, collapsed to the ground. The air seemed to thicken with an otherworldly malevolence, and the specter of Virote's demise lingered like a haunting wail. The battlefield, once a stage for epic confrontation, was now a canvas painted with the horrors of the supernatural.

As Hakana stood amidst the surreal aftermath, the weight of his actions settled upon him like an oppressive fog. The divine blade, now in his grasp, whispered of a history written in blood, its malevolent aura a constant reminder of the darkness that had once controlled him. The shadows of the fallen Demon General, Virote, continued to cast a haunting pall over the accursed battleground.

Sun Wukong approached Hakana, his wise eyes reflecting a blend of empathy and understanding. "I'm proud of you, Hakana. You have demonstrated greatness today."

Hakana nodded, The Monkey King placed a reassuring hand on Hakana's shoulder. "We stand together, united against the forces that threaten this world."

As the realization of the broader conflict settled in, Sun Wukong, Hakana, and the others gathered. The remnants of the Gnok Army still lingered, their influence seeping into the very land they had desecrated. The four, bound by a common purpose, began to discuss plans for healing and strategizing to diminish the other demon hives that plagued the lands. Hakana, having tasted the bitter fruit of enslavement, was determined to liberate others from a similar fate.

The surreal aftermath of the battle served as a stark reminder that this was just the beginning. The journey ahead would be arduous, and the shadows of the fallen would continue to cast their long reach over the lands. Yet, with newfound allies and a resolve born from the crucible of conflict, they faced the future together—a future where the echoes of General Virote's demise were but a prelude to a greater struggle for the soul of the realm. The group turned their eyes toward the horizon, ready to embark on a quest to reclaim the lands and bring an end to the demonic tyranny that plagued their world.